CHAPTER ONE

London, England
Thursday, March 27
11:14 p.m.

My name is Becca Moore, and I'm—*tick, tick*—a time bomb.

Now, if I were a funny person, just saying I'm a *time bomb* would be pretty hilarious. Like ha-ha-ha and your head falls off. But I'm not a funny person.

To prove it, I'll tell you what I did today. Straight from the beginning, through the bloody noses, the actual heads coming off, the mysterious black BMW, the blind man with a torch, and all the way to the falling man. Men. Falling men.

Unfunny. Truly.

Except maybe for the exploding rental car. That was a minor riot. Not for Archie Doyle, of course, but

1

then, he was trying to kill us at the time, so he probably deserved it. Anyway, you decide what's funny and what's not. It's nighttime now, but I'll start with this morning, a little more than twelve hours ago, and the old boat by the river.

London. End of March. Ten thirty-something a.m. Gray sky. Cool, not cold, with a light, sprinkling rain. But it's England, so what do you expect? Sunshine was promised for later, and it came eventually. But not here, not this morning.

They were all with me—Wade Kaplan; his cousin Lily; his stepbrother, Darrell; Darrell's mom, Sara; Wade's father, Roald. Next to my family, these are the people I love most in the world.

Julian Ackroyd was there, too. Julian is the son of the superrich writer Terence Ackroyd, who is helping us search for the relics. Julian was the one who met us at Westminster Abbey this morning and told us about the boat they dug up at the river. And how Galina Krause's personal archaeologist, Markus Wolff, was spotted snooping around it.

I know I'm telling this way too fast. That's because my heart is hammering my ribs, I'm shaking like a leaf, and I have to get the story out before it's too late. Except that by now, after staring down from the top of an old

2

church tower at night, I know that it's already too late, though it wasn't yet, not this morning.

I know, I know, I get it. This is a mess. I'll try to slow down.

Breathe, Becca. Breathe.

So . . . Julian's limo dropped us off on Lower Thames Street, not too far from the Tower of London. If you look at a map, you'll see where I'm talking about. We were near the Cannon Street Underground station. We hadn't seen the black car yet. We eased down the gentle slope of streets between the financial buildings to a place named Hanseatic Walk. There are lots of "walks" along the river. This one meant nothing to me this morning. It meant everything later on.

By the time we reached the Thames, a big crowd had gathered on the embankment. The river is a wide green snake that slithers through the heart of London, splitting it in two. You can see that on maps, too.

"How did they discover the boat?" Wade asked Julian as we pressed closer.

"A city repair crew testing the drains uncovered the remains yesterday," Julian told us. "They called archaeologists right away, who have already found traces of amber. First report is that the cargo might have been amber from the Baltic. Maybe early sixteenth century."

Julian is a few years older than us, seventeen, has

long blond hair, is handsome, and is very techy, like Lily. As if to prove it, they each took out their phones and tablets and snapped pictures while the rest of us just gawked.

The narrow stretch of sand below the embankment wall had already been transformed into a makeshift archaeological site. A waist-high wall of sandbags was set around the site to keep the water back, while inside the perimeter a grid of wooden stakes had been pounded into the ground, with strings woven among the stakes to form a section of perfect squares. The tidiness of the past.

Tidiness? Maybe I am funny. Ha-ha.

"Slews of city officials, government types, and sightseers have all swarmed down here to see what's been found," Julian said, jostling for a better view.

"It might have been a flat-bottomed boat discovered here," Roald said, trying to see over the heads. Between us and the dig site there could have been two hundred people or more. "Barges are a big part of Thames traffic, aren't they?"

"Absolutely," said Julian. He knew because he'd lived in London. "Larger ships dock downriver. Barges have always brought cargo to and from the city."

Darrell nodded slowly. "Copernicus lived on the Baltic Sea. If Markus Wolff is interested in this barge, then Galina Krause and the Order are interested. And if *they're* involved, it's got to be part of the relic hunt."

Relic hunt? Markus Wolff? Galina Krause? Copernicus? The Order?

Sorry. Time for some background. The basic facts are simple enough.

Five hundred years ago, the Polish astronomer Nicolaus Copernicus discovered, rebuilt, rode around in, and then took apart an amazing machine, a kind of large astrolabe with seats. Why? Because the astrolabe had the power to travel through time. If you don't believe that yet, you will.

When Albrecht von Hohenzollern, the Grand Master of the murderous Knights of the Teutonic Order—you'll hear that name a lot—got wind of his time travels, Copernicus set out to hide the twelve most important parts of the astrolabe—he called them *relics*.

The main reason we know all of this is because a couple of long weeks ago we discovered Copernicus's secret diary in a private fencing school in Italy. The diary is written in several languages as well as a ton of codes and riddles. Thanks to my grandparents, I know a few languages, and I've been able to translate some of the words. The codes are more Wade's territory.

Anyway, for five long centuries, Copernicus's friends

the Guardians (and *their* friends and descendants) kept the twelve astrolabe relics pretty well hidden.

Unfortunately, a crazy woman named Galina Krause—the nineteen-year-old current leader of the Teutonic Order—murdered a major Guardian, who turned out to be Wade's old uncle Henry. Now we're Guardians, too.

"Becca, you're rocking again." Lily held my arm to steady me.

Right. I'd found myself rocking on my heels a lot lately. It calmed me. Lily calmed me. Wade is an intense math guy and star lover like his father, and Darrell has flashes of brilliance in the middle of certifiable looni-ness, but Lily is, of all of them, closest to me. Not only is she an amazing tech brain, with a superquick mind, but she cares about me and from the start has always been there for me.

"Sorry," I told her. "I'm still recovering from Grey-wolf."

Greywolf? Now we're getting to the time-bomb thing.

Twelve days ago, Galina Krause kidnapped Darrell's mom, Sara Kaplan. Galina smuggled her into Russia and caged her inside the Order's own experimental time-travel device, Kronos, a scary machine based on Galina's design. I know, a nineteen-year-old building a time machine? But Galina is brilliant and she did.

I found out the hard way that Kronos sort of actually worked.

"You're going to have to tell me *exactly* what happened at Greywolf," Lily said with a noticeable shiver. "Every detail. Because you changed. I know you don't want to think you changed, but you did. I mean, you're still great and all, but you're different. Quieter, if that's possible. Farther away. Since Greywolf."

"But you don't have to worry about it—"

"I·get to worry if I want to," she snapped, her eyes locked on mine like a pair of laser beams. That's the other thing. I really can't lie to her. She can always tell.

"You're right. Sorry."

"And stop apologizing!" she growled. "It's me, remember?"

"Okay, okay. I didn't mean that. I'm sor . . . *not* sorry."

"That's right you're not. Now, help me get closer." She nudged forward.

At Greywolf Galina tried to use Kronos to zap Sara back to the sixteenth century to check on Copernicus and find out where the original Guardians hid the twelve relics. Insane, sure. But Galina's plan nearly worked.

Luckily, we rescued Sara at the very instant Kronos went off.

Unluckily, the machine blasted Helmut Bern full

in the face. He's one of the Order's scientists. Instantly, both Bern and the machine vanished.

Unluckiest of all—for me, at least—was that I was zapped by Kronos, too.

Now I'm able to *see* Helmut Bern five hundred years in the past. Bizarre, I know. I mean, I'm not going *physically* into the past with him.

I'm only going back in time *in my mind*.

And only in *blackouts*.

Only.

Since Kronos blasted me, I'd clocked out a few times. I hadn't told anybody, because I kept hoping the blackouts would just go away.

But they weren't going away. After the last time in Westminster Abbey this morning, it was clear that they were getting worse. And I couldn't seem to tell—*tick, tick*—when they'd happen again and blast me into the past.

So you see . . . I'm a time bomb.

"It would be great to spy on Markus Wolff for a change," Wade whispered. As he scanned the crowd, he ran his fingers through his rain-sprinkled hair, then dried his hand on his jeans. "But we can't see anything from here."

"Mom, Dad," said Darrell, "can we sneak in for a better look at the dig?"

"I think we need to, Uncle Roald," said Lily. "If

you-know-who is involved."

Roald and Sara were a few feet behind us, talking quietly to each other. He stood on his tiptoes and searched the crowd for suspicious faces.

"Don't go far," he said. "Julian, please go with them. We'll be right here."

The crowd was too thick to let Sara through, so Roald stayed, holding tightly to her wheelchair handles. She'd been in the chair since the hospital yesterday. Her kidnapping had exhausted her. But she was getting her strength back.

"Kids, be careful," Sara said. "Use your alarms and we'll come running. And rolling." Sara had bought us each a souvenir at the abbey gift shop, a key chain of a stained-glass window that we could beep if we felt threatened. Of course, after the boys had hooked the alarms on their belt loops, they'd kept pressing them until Sara snapped, "They're not toys!"

"Okay, Mom," Darrell said now. "We'll be smart, even Beep. I mean Wade."

Darrell and Julian pushed carefully ahead through the bunched-up spectators. Wade tagged along with Lily and me. He wasn't smiling.

Does he already know that something's going on with me? He's always looking *at me. I'll have to tell everyone sooner or later, but later sounds good.*

Not until I have to.

"The Romans settled London," Julian said over his shoulder. "They called it Londinium. This neighborhood here is now the financial heart of the city."

Which was useful to know, but as we wormed away from the Hanseatic Walk, I couldn't keep my eyes off the faces. Everyone we passed seemed suspicious. I checked each face against my memory of a killer we called Umbrella Man. He was a doughy guy who wore disguises and used a poison-tipped umbrella to murder Guardians. I scanned the throng for a toupee or fake mustache.

"I can see the boat!" Lily pointed over the embankment to a framework of black planks in the sand. "Uncle Roald was right. It does look like a—"

I didn't hear the rest. The moment I actually set my eyes on the remains of the barge, a bolt of rainy light flashed off the water, and I felt a chill run up my back.

No, please no. I'd felt the same chill before each blackout. My breath left me, and my vision darkened and narrowed, as if I were going to faint. My head began to pound. I pressed the balls of my feet hard against the ground and clutched at Lily's arm to keep hold of myself, but it was too late.

The silver light rippled across the river again, then winked out entirely. I was plunged into darkness as if somebody flipped a switch. The buzz of the crowd vanished. The traffic's roar shut off. I heard hooves—horse hooves!—clomping up the streets behind me. Men called out in English and German.

I spun around, gasping. "Lily, Wade, I—I—"

But it was too late. *Tick*.

They couldn't hear me. *Tick. Tick.*

I wasn't there anymore.

CHAPTER TWO

Light flared violently on the wet sand below me. A torch. A face materialized behind it. The flame moved, and two more torches were born. I watched the first one bob up away from the water and vanish into the streets. All this time there were voices of men shouting, grunting in labor.

A flat-bottomed boat—*this same* barge, the one we'd been studying seconds before—was no longer a skeleton, but was hulled and half decked and stacked with cargo and crawling with men in britches and tunics and boots and cloaks. Among the barrels and crates, a shape twitched. His face caught the moonlight.

My heart stopped. I knew him. "Omigod . . ."

It was Helmut Bern. Victim of Kronos. Scientist of the Teutonic Order.

I so wanted Lily, Wade, and Darrell to see all this with me, but they weren't here. I wasn't clear if anyone I saw could see or hear me.

Bern clawed his way from the boat, crying out in inarticulate German. His eyes were jammed closed, as if he were tortured by a headache as piercing as mine. His arms, visible through his shredded robes—he was dressed a little like a monk—were all wounds and sores. Boils, maybe? I don't really know what boils are.

Then—I have no idea how—I was on the sand next to him.

This is soooo insane! I told myself. *I have to wake up! Becca, wake up! Someone—wake—me—up!*

But the more I tried, the more I couldn't wake up. Huge, modern London had simply disappeared. No more clogged traffic and skyscrapers and steel office buildings and banks and luxury hotels. Now there were sloping fields of grass, and trees and timbered houses poking up where big buildings had just been, and dirt and cobblestoned paths in place of paved streets, and the deep darkness of a sky filled with more stars than I had ever seen.

In the near distance stood the famous Tower of

London. It's still there today. Back then—the year Kronos was set to travel to—the Tower was the largest structure for miles, a massive block of white stone with corner towers, surrounded by a high wall. It loomed over the whole rambling city, an oppressive presence. Not the palace I'd read it began life as but a horrible, sorrow-filled prison.

Helmut Bern convulsed on the sand and rolled over onto his hands and knees. He lifted his head to the moonlight and gave out a cry like a dying animal. Ignoring him, the other boatmen climbed, grunting, into the streets behind me. They called to one another—also in German.

Bern was teetering on his feet now and stumbling from the barge toward a path sloping up from the river, staggering from wall to wall to keep from falling.

"Helmut Bern?" I found myself saying. It was weird. Bern was the only person I knew there. And even though he had tried to kill Sara—and me—his was a face I knew. It's funny how a familiar face means more when you're lost.

I moved toward him, raising my hand to get his attention—"Bern? Helmut?"—when a man barreled past, accidentally brushing my arm where Galina had shot me with a crossbow. It ached for a second, and it startled me that I could *feel* anything in this dream, but I shook off the pain.

The man who had rushed by was tall and broad-shouldered. He wore a long, thick cloak, forest green, and a black velvet hat. I remembered seeing him in an earlier blackout, when Bern and I were being sick over the side of the sailing ship. This man now slid his arm under Bern's shoulder, spoke to him in German. *"Lassen Sie mich Ihnen helfen. Bitte kommen Sie mit."* (Let me help you. Please come with me.)

They struggled up and away from the water to where I'd heard the horses clomping and wagon wheels screeching. A thick smell like an open sewer filled my nose. It was awful, but I followed after the men, knowing—somehow—that I wasn't *really* going any-where. I'd discovered that while I blacked out, I didn't actually leave the place where I was. And no matter how long my visions seemed to keep me in the past, pretty much no time passed in the present.

A child's voice called out suddenly in the night. A girl's voice.

"This way, please. Father is waiting for you!"

The girl stood at the end of a lane, holding a lantern. She wore a shawl over her shoulders, and when a sudden breeze ruffled her bonnet, the ends of her hair coiled up behind her. "This way!" I glanced at the signpost nearest me. Allhallows Lane. I hurried to keep pace with Bern and the green-cloaked man. The girl waved to them. Her face told me she might be eleven or twelve years old. Nearly my age. The lantern's light shone warmly on her cheeks.

"Meg," boomed a man I couldn't see. "Meg! Where are you?"

"Here, Father!" The girl—Meg—turned and vanished, drawing the wobbly light of her lantern around the corner of Allhallows. Still unseen, I followed the men street after street until we came to a short cobbled passage.

I read the signpost. "Bucklersbury," I said aloud. My voice was muffled.

The other sailors had split off. It was only the girl and the three of us—if I could even think of myself as one of them. We went left onto Bucklersbury, and I saw the girl on the doorstep of a long, low, rambling building. "Our house is called the Old Barge, sirs. You see why!" The door opened from the inside.

I wanted Wade and everyone to see this with me.

"Father is waiting for you," Meg said, waving in Bern and the man with the green cloak, whom I now saw carried a leather pack over his shoulder. Just before Meg closed the door, I slipped inside and followed them into a warm, dry room.

The room had a low ceiling, and the air smelled of burning wood and too many people and the warm aroma of baking bread. All the scents combined into a strange kind of potion, and I felt my tensed-up muscles begin to relax.

A man in a simple long robe and soft shoes swept into the room. *"Nam blandit quam ut domus!"* he said, his arms open wide. It was something like "Welcome to our house." "I am Thomas. At your service."

"I am Nicolaus," said the man in green, embracing Thomas. "This fellow is a stranger, and I fear he is quite ill."

I stopped breathing. Nicolaus. He pulled off his hat, and I caught his face for the first time as he turned to the hearth fire. Nicolaus. It couldn't really be.

Except that it was.

I knew him from his famous self-portrait. He was dressed in many layers, with tights beneath his robes that were like thick leggings. Cold had rosied his cheeks and the backs of his hands. He placed his bag down and threw off his cloak.

The man standing in front of me, as real as life, was Nicolaus Copernicus.

CHAPTER THREE

"Meg, dear, call your stepmother, please," said the man named Thomas. "Nicolaus and I will help our poor friend into the next room."

Shivering, I moved aside and watched, amazed, as Copernicus and Thomas helped Helmut Bern toward a long daybed. The whole time, Bern bled from his nose and stared wildly about like he was crazy.

No one in the room saw me. I felt like a spy, lurking in that house. I knew I wasn't *physically there back then*, but Bern obviously was, and he was in bad shape, convulsing, twitching, barely able to stand.

Sara would have been the same if we hadn't rescued her in time.

Together Nicolaus and Thomas laid Helmut Bern

down and covered him with a rough-knitted blanket. Then several women in plain long dresses and bonnets appeared from a back room. One of them balanced a basin that brimmed with steaming water, another an armful of cloths. Meg trailed them, holding a brown ceramic mug of something hot.

I stood in the corner, barely breathing, while Thomas led Copernicus to a smaller room. I followed them, knowing I was invisible, but tiptoeing for fear of making a sound. They sat together at a small candlelit table. Thomas brushed his hand across the table as if sweeping away invisible crumbs.

"In the morning," he said, "we will take your friend to Charterhouse. A hospital. I will support his care until he recovers. They will know best how to treat his ailment."

"He is less a friend than a stowaway," Nicolaus said in thickly accented English, but softly, as if not wanting Bern to hear. "He came aboard in the Netherlands in a monk's robe, but says he is not a monk. Sadly, I fear the man is doomed. This may be leprosy that he suffers. My brother, Andreas, has it."

"Ah . . ." Thomas trailed off. When he spoke again, his voice was quiet, too. "I received your letter, Magister. I will do as much as I can and tell no one. Except perhaps Margaret, who is very close to me. Look, here she is. Meg, come meet our guest properly. Nicolaus Copernicus is an astronomer of great renown."

"Like Herr Kratzer?" said Meg, with a curtsy. She smiled, and her cheeks dimpled. I liked her right away. Meg was Margaret. Just like my sister, Maggie.

Copernicus turned to Thomas. "Are you saying Kratzer is here?"

"He teaches my daughters. The German community is large in London. Meg, our guest is far more famous than Herr Kratzer. Believe me."

"Oh, I do!" She curtsied again. "I always do, Father!"

I felt stupid, not knowing who these people were. Thomas. Meg. Herr Kratzer. I had to remember everything and decrypt it later. Lily would help me by searching online for answers. I *hoped* Lily would help me. *If* I ever got back to the present. And *if* anyone believed that my fevered brain hadn't made all this up.

Meg tugged a sheet of paper from a pocket in her dress and set it on the table. "Father, did I do it properly?"

Thomas held the sheet to the candle. I leaned over to see. In a small, neat script was a series of strange letters.

⊙☺▢△⊙⌐

"Yes, very good, Meg," her father said. "Nicely formed."

"What is this?" Copernicus asked. "A secret language between you two?"

"A playful code I invented for my latest little book," Thomas said, tugging a slim volume from a shelf behind him. He handed it to the astronomer, who opened it to the beginning and ran his finger along a page I couldn't see.

Copernicus studied the characters on Meg's paper, then the book, and smiled. "I see, yes. If I may . . . here are more words to decipher." Glancing back and forth from the book to Meg's paper, he picked up a quill that lay on the table, dipped it into a brass ink bottle, and wrote four words in the odd characters.

ⵁⵔⵛⵟⵟⵟ ⵎⵎⵏⵟⵛⵏⵟⵏⵔⵟ△
ⵎⵟⵟⵛⵟⵟ ⵁⵏⵟⵎⵎⵏⵟⵟ△ⵛ

I stared at the "letters" to memorize them. Three circles with lines in various places, three boxes with lines, a small *c*, three letters that looked like *LOL*, something like the French cookie called a *macaron*, another *l*, a backward *c*, a dome, a box with a dot, a triangle.

"I'll decode them right now!" she said, taking the paper from him.

"But listen, Meg," said Nicolaus. "The first two words are for your sister Elizabeth to decipher. The other two

21

are for you, yes? Remember these words. They will be important to you in, oh, about ten years."

"Ten years? What do you mean, sir?" she asked.

Nicolaus smiled. "In ten years a good man will come to paint your picture. And, oh, yes, tell Elizabeth not to kick the sleeping dog!"

What *that* meant, I had no idea. But Meg laughed and scooted away to another room, leaving the two men alone—with me.

"She is my dearest," Thomas said softly.

"I know. I can see the way you two trade glances. And now . . ."

Copernicus removed a wooden box from his sack. He unclasped the leather strap binding it and opened the lid away from himself. A rich yellow light flashed from the box onto both of their faces. Thomas shielded his eyes. "My goodness!"

"It is amber, already a thousand years old. Older," Nicolaus said. "When my friend the artist does come to you, have him build a better box to hide it in. This is soaked by seawater. Seal this item's two equal arms separately, or, believe me, they will overwhelm you. Thomas, I tell you, this object, like so many of its brothers, is terribly dangerous."

I was confused by "two equal arms," but I knew I was seeing an incredible thing—Copernicus in the very

22

act of transferring a relic to a Guardian. To Thomas. But to Thomas *who*?

I tried to edge around, but I feared I might make a sound, so I never saw what was inside the box, only the bright golden light that shone out of it. Thomas took the box and closed the lid. The room darkened as before to dull candlelight.

"*Voteo facio quod possum,*" he whispered. "*Cujuscumque periculum.*"

I promised myself to remember the Latin, even though I know only some of the words. But I already guessed their meaning: "Upon my life I will." The vow that every Guardian makes. The promise to protect the relic to the end.

Just then a tiny black-haired girl in a blue tunic peeked around the corner at the two men. She was very young. Two years old, maybe, or even less. But she was beautiful, with the sweetest pink face and rosy lips, and deep, dark eyes that seemed to glow like coals. She made a noise in her throat as she toddled into the room, clutched the hem of Thomas's robe, and tugged it, grumbling happily.

"But who is this little angel?" Copernicus held his arms open. She ran to him.

"Alas, a foundling," Thomas said. "The poor child suffers from an unnamed wound and cannot speak a word. But her eyes are language enough, yes? We call her Joan Aleyn. She is as dear to me as are my own daughters."

A bell rang twice in a distant room.

"Ah, a courier from the king. Business calls me," Thomas said, standing. He smiled, then grew serious. The light in the room seemed to focus on his face, and the lines around his eyes gave him a look of pain. "I promise, my friend, until my dying breath, to do as you ask. Stay here for now. Come, Joan. Let us see what your sisters are up to, yes?"

Thomas took up the wooden box, snatched the tiny girl into his arms, and drifted into another room, leaving the great astronomer alone.

Copernicus followed Thomas with his eyes. I didn't breathe. He leaned back at the table; then he let out a deep sigh. He dipped into his satchel once more and took out what I knew instantly was his secret diary— the diary that at that very moment was in my own bag!

He stared at the book's leather cover and brass corner ornaments. They were far less worn than they would be five centuries later. He turned to a clean page. He picked up Thomas's pen and dipped it again in the inkwell.

I felt alone, so alone, among all these dead people. I wanted to get back to the others, to today, to wake up from this dream, or whatever it was, and forget it.

But a voice in my head said, *Not yet.*

I had to admit that since our relic hunt began, I'd come to know Nicolaus Copernicus as I knew my own friends. I wanted to talk to him, to open my bag and show him what I had. I wanted to scream to him:

Do you know what my friends and I are doing? We're Guardians just like your friend Thomas!

I burned to see what page he was writing on, so that I might read it later—the page he wrote while I stood near him. I moved closer, an inch maybe, no more. The candle's flame quavered, as if the air was disturbed. Surely not by me. I was a ghost. Copernicus lifted his eyes from the page and observed the flame wobbling. I breathed as silently as I could. Still, the flame's tongue reacted, as if the air around me had rippled.

Copernicus set down his pen.

He turned his face to me.

"Rebecca Moore," he said.

CHAPTER FOUR

My vision went black around the edges. My heart pounded as if it would explode. But I held on to myself. I bit my lip, felt my feet on the floor, and focused. I was still afraid to take a step out of the shadows.

"You're Copernicus? You're really him? How can I . . . how . . . ?"

"Let us not waste time on these things, Rebecca Moore." His voice deepened suddenly. "We have a few moments only. Yes, this is London. Yes, it is November of the year 1517. By some trick—or gift—that I do not understand, travelers such as we can see each other. I am here, but these others cannot see you."

"So what am I, a ghost?" I said.

He waved that away. "I know, of course, what will

happen to my friend Thomas, though I must not tell him. The horror of knowing and not being able to warn, the horror of knowing it will happen anyway. This is why, you see, we use codes. To hide the truth—not only from the Teutonic Order. But from ourselves."

The candlelight warmed his face, as the fire in the hearth must have warmed him, though I saw him shiver. I tried to shape my thoughts. I couldn't.

"For Thomas," he said, "it will happen in eighteen short years."

"What will happen to him?"

"A rise in fortunes, then a fall. Friendships with King Henry seldom end well. Thomas will be executed on the sixth of July in 1535. Everyone knows this in your time."

I felt my head emptying out, like water going down a drain. I was faint, ready to fall to the ground, to fall somewhere, but Copernicus rose quickly, took hold of me by my arms, and settled me in a chair. I didn't think it was possible to have form and weight in a dream. Maybe I imagined that, too.

He stood, his forehead deeply furrowed. "Rebecca Moore, I bear much guilt. Perhaps I am guilty even of *this*." He glanced to the other room. "A time traveler is like a blind man with a torch, setting fire to everything he stumbles into."

My mouth was as dry as sand. "What do you mean? How can traveling in time do that?" I wished Wade could have heard this, to understand the *time* thing.

"Time travelers are sleepwalkers," he said. "We trail destruction behind us. Accidental murderers. This is why I took the astrolabe apart. I saw what I had done. What more horrors *could* be done by the Order. Do you see now?"

"I don't see. I don't understand—"

He seemed upset. "Horrible things happen when you travel this way!" He waved his hand up and down to signify—what?—a passage through time? "I didn't know this until my second journey. The holes we created, the holes we left behind. The first journey was joy I'd never known! Rebecca, there was beauty and wonder everywhere, and yes, the blessed power of good!" His eyes sparkled, then faded. "The second time, no. I saw what horrors I had begun."

I was getting so little of what he told me. "What horrors *you* had begun? But you wouldn't have. You're good. How? And how many journeys did you make?"

"Whenever one travels this way, a hole is created," he said. "In your time you will know it as a nuclear event."

It was strange to hear a man in an old house in London in the sixteenth century use the word *nuclear*.

"In this time"—he spread his hands wide—"it is seen as a hole in the sky, a hole as narrow as a dagger's point." I remembered reading those words in the diary. "Things drift that should not," he said. "*People* drift, sometimes."

"But you can do good things because of traveling in time, can't you?" I asked. "Something good must happen. It must."

He was quiet for the longest time before he said, "She lives."

"Who?" I said. "Who lives?"

"But because she lives . . . there is *the evil*. You cannot escape that. . . ."

He trailed off.

When I pleaded with him to tell me more, he shook his head sharply. "I should not. I cannot. You must return. Go back. Do not come here again, Rebecca Moore. The evil, the loneliness will break you, do you see?"

"Stop saying that! I don't see! What are you trying to tell me?"

He turned his face to the fire, overcome by something, then said, "To find this relic, remember the words I gave to Meg. Serpens does not lead to it. The words I gave to Thomas's daughter are for you, too."

"I don't know the code—"

"It has to be in code! To tell you outright would be far more dangerous."

"Why?" I was getting angry, too. "Why?"

"Because you would stop searching! You cannot stop searching! Look here." He spun the diary around to the page he had written on while I stood in the shadows. What he had inked were four more words with the odd characters.

○⊟L △L▢▢⊟○ ⊟△⊕▢○○ ▢⊟⊟▢○△

"Can't you just tell me what it means?" I pleaded.

"This—*this*—will happen after nightfall tonight."

"After nightfall tonight? *Whose* night? Yours or mine?"

My brain was fizzling out. Too much information. The horror of knowing, his second journey, the bizarre codes, the sleepwalker.

Then as I stared at the page, trying to etch the symbols into my mind, Nicolaus whispered into my ear, "The . . . Temple . . . of . . . Mithras . . ."

I wanted to ask what he meant, but my words were lost in a mist. Whether he began to fade away from me or I from him, it didn't matter. Without my leaving that close, hot, shivering room, I was dragged away from him, from the old house and the old city, and I couldn't see him anymore.

CHAPTER FIVE

"Wolff is on the embankment. I see him. Becca, stay here with us."

The hand was gentle but insistent, tugging me backward. I turned, and there was Wade's face. The Old Barge was gone. Bucklersbury was gone. The ancient curving street was replaced by the throng at the river. Rain sprinkled my face. It was this morning again. Wade and Lily huddled close on either side of me, while Darrell stood in front, as if blocking us from being seen.

"Becca, pay attention!" Lily's voice in my ear.

"What? Sorry."

"I told you not to say that."

The half hour, or longer, that I had been back *there* with Helmut Bern and Meg and Thomas and Nicolaus had gone by in an instant. I was barely a step or two from where I'd been when everything winked out and I saw Helmut Bern crawling on the sand.

"He's moving." Darrell nodded back over his shoulder.

I saw him then, Markus Wolff. A tall man with a craggy face and close-cropped white hair, walking slowly among those gathered on the far side of the excavation. His black overcoat—the one that had gained him Lily's nickname Leathercoat—glistened in the light rain. Seeing him, remembering how he'd threatened us at gunpoint in San Francisco, shocked me back to the here and now.

As Wolff trained his icy eyes on the workers below and took snapshots with his phone, my time with Nicolaus seemed to snuff out like a candle in the rain.

"He's sending pictures to Galina," Wade murmured.

"It's strange to see Wolff in the daylight, isn't it?" Lily whispered. "He's so like a vampire, except that vampires are hilarious compared to him."

My head was splitting. "Just what I was thinking," I managed to say. The area behind my eyes ached; so did my jaw, as if I'd been clenching my teeth too long. My nose was running, too. When I wiped it, my finger was smeared with blood.

With blood! Like Helmut Bern! I turned away from

everyone, but that was it. A single drop. I wiped my finger on my jeans.

We started back to Roald and Sara, when all at once the crowd lurched and parted. A long black car, just this side of being a limousine, pushed through the spectators, nudging them away. It stopped.

"BMW," said Darrell. "And it has no license plates. Julian, no plates."

A tall man in a dark raincoat with a slouchy rain hat pulled low over his face exited the rear of the car. He stepped to the edge of the embankment.

"Government, maybe," Julian said. "Or royal family, checking out the barge."

Wolff turned his gaze from the barge to the hatted man and watched his movements down to the sand as steadily as I followed Wolff's. The work stopped, while the man in the hat spoke to a couple of archaeologists, one of whom was nodding, the other of whom seemed to be almost angry. The man raised his hand, turned away, and answered his phone. He spoke a few words into it. I looked back at Wolff. He was on the phone, too.

"They're talking to each other," I said. "That man down there is working for the Order."

"We'll call him Hatman," Lily said.

Wade ran his hand through his wet hair again. "If he is with the Order, he's high up in the government, right? Someone who doesn't need license plates."

While Wolff kept speaking on his phone, Hatman scanned the crowd, moving his gaze nearer and nearer to us.

"Get back—he's looking for us," said Roald, tugging us into the ranks of the spectators so we couldn't be seen. At the same time, two hefty-size gargoyles emerged from the black BMW. They were dressed in black jeans and jackets. They'd seen us. They entered the crowd and moved toward us.

Sara stood from her wheelchair. "Julian, I think we need our car now. Let's get away from here."

"I'm calling for it," said Julian. "I don't know who those men are."

Several policemen barked at the spectators to move back from the BMW. It reversed slowly, leaving the two gargoyles behind. My head thundered. What was happening? I could faint at any second. My nostril was damp. I sniffed it in.

"We need to vanish." Roald urged us through the fringes of the crowd and away from the embankment. Sara was back in the chair. Darrell pushed as quickly as he could—"Excuse, please!"—and helped make a path for us.

Julian swiped off his phone. "Our driver can't make it around the crowds. He'll meet us on Upper

Thames Street, straight ahead—"

Everything ached, as if I'd fallen down a long flight of stairs, but I pushed ahead with the others; then I looked up, and saw the street sign.

Allhallows Lane. The path taken by Bern and Copernicus.

I shivered all over, but my face and neck burned. "Uh . . ."

"Come on, Bec," Lily said, pulling my arm. "Julian knows the best way."

I stopped. If the twisting old streets were still there, we could avoid the mysterious car with no license plates, maybe put the two thugs off the scent.

"This way," I said. It was how the girl, Meg, had said it. "This way."

"Becca, no," said Wade. "Where do you think you're—"

I pulled away from the others, trotted down some stairs, and turned left off Allhallows, through a tunnel marked with blue lights on the pavement. Parked motorcycles lined the tunnel. Then right, up the hill away from the river. Yes. This was the way.

"Becca, wait," Roald said from the back. "The wheelchair."

Sara, too. "Becca, we can't—"

But Julian said, "No. Let me help you down the

stairs. Becca's right. This is better. I'll phone my driver. Everyone follow her."

Soot-black walls rose up narrowly on either side of me. The street ahead was lined with trucks, blocking other vehicles from entering. It was the same path, the same corner. So I *hadn't* dreamed it. It *had* been real, my climb from the river through the streets after Helmut Bern. After Copernicus.

Suddenly Wade was running with me, past a couple of old cannons—of Cannon Street? Lily was there, too. There might have been a more direct way, but when I saw the old, narrow path of College Street, I entered it. Just like I had five hundred years ago.

Darrell pushed his mother as quickly as he could. The streets were bumpy, barely paved over centuries of cobblestones. "Hold up," he called.

"No! Follow me!" I passed a church on the right, then rounded another corner up and away from the river. "Just follow me."

"The men," Roald said from the back. "The men from the black car . . ."

We forged up College Hill, then down and left onto Walbrook and up into Bucklersbury Passage, where the Old Barge had stood ages ago. The BMW was suddenly roaring up the nearest passable street and skidded across one end of the passage. A motorcycle stopped at the other end. In its saddle was one of the goons in black jeans. Where had he picked up a bike? In the tunnel with blue lights?

"We need to move faster," said Darrell. "Mom?"

She got out of the chair with Roald's help. "I'm good. Really. Let's go."

A second motorcycle joined the first, idling with it. Both engines cut out at the same time. The riders dismounted together.

My legs felt like collapsing. I stumbled. Lily kept up with me. "Becca, really, what's going on with you? You have to tell me. You've never been here before."

"Not now," I said. "I just know the way. That's all."

"Sure. Okay."

I knew it was wrong to keep this to myself. The loneliness of it *would* break me. Nicolaus knew it. That was the real horror. To be left alone in a cold place without my friends. Only myself. No others. Suddenly I froze. There was a fence surrounding a construction site. A sign pinned up on it read Temple of Mithras.

"The temple!" I said. "He told me about it."

"The temple?" Julian shot a look at me, then behind us. The two motorcycle men had joined two or three others on foot now. I saw Hatman's hand pointing out the car window.

"Through the fence to the next block," Julian said.

"Becca's right. Go!"

Wade and Darrell pushed at a hinged door in the fence and urged Lily and me through it, then Roald and Sara. Julian ran in last, still on the phone to his driver, who must be trying desperately to find us.

We wove through cranes and tractors, piles of girders, and shouting construction workers—"Hey, it's not open yet!" "Get out of here!" "Bloody tourists!"—and finally past the red and white foundation stones of an ancient temple nestled serenely among the noise and fenced off within the fenced-off site. We crashed out to the street a block away from the men at the exact moment that Julian's limo raced up the street toward us.

Wade faltered. "Becca, what the—how in the world did you know—"

"I'll tell you!" I said. "I'll tell you everything! Just get in!"

Breathless, we dived into the car, Julian pulling the doors closed behind us. The limo screeched away from the curb, and the moment it did, I did tell them.

Almost everything.

CHAPTER SIX

The car raced north through the streets as I blabbed. My nose may have bled again, another drop, but I wiped it away before anyone saw. I told them about the blackouts, the barge, Helmut Bern, Thomas and Nicolaus, the code he wrote in the diary, Meg's codes, the horror, and whatever else I could remember.

They sat there stunned until I finished. Then they just sat there.

"I'm sorry I kept it a secret," I said. "I didn't want to, except I wasn't sure it was anything real. But I knew the way up the streets, and he told me 'the Temple of Mithras,' which I had never heard of, and our car was exactly there. He knew it would be, don't ask me how, but he knew!"

Roald frowned deeply and seemed on the verge of speaking, while Sara studied my face and held my hand calmly. In the end, it was Wade who spoke.

"Are you saying . . . you actually *saw* him? You *talked* to him? To *Copernicus*? The real guy? And he *knew* you?" He stared into my eyes as deeply as he ever had. "I can't believe you really *talked* to *him*—"

"Seriously, Wade?" Lily snapped. "Becca flies away to the sixteenth century and might never come back, and *that's* what you can't believe? Not that oh, poor Becca might be going nuts? Not that you're going nuts," she said to me. "I'm just saying."

"Yeah, but Copernicus!" said Wade, shaking his head. "Him himself! It's just . . . hard to believe."

"She knew the way," said Darrell. "I believe her."

We motored past a giant domed church. I remembered from our first time in London that it was the famous Saint Paul's Cathedral.

"It *is* hard to believe," I said. "I just hope I'm really *not* going nuts."

Sara stroked my hand. "You're not. When Kronos exploded, that did this to you. The machine and her, Galina." Her eyes narrowed in disgust. "But I'm sure it won't last. It's like post-traumatic stress. It'll fade."

I felt like collapsing in her arms. I thought of my mother, father, and Maggie, and how I wanted this to be over by the time they all got here. But the blackouts, or whatever they were, seemed to be getting longer and deeper for me.

"Thanks," I said. "I think I'm okay now. It's just . . . very . . . weird."

"At least you didn't disappear," Darrell said. "It's all in your head."

"It is not, Darrell!" said Lily, my guard dog again. "It's real!"

"What I mean is," he said patiently, "you were still here when your brain threw you back in time. It would be so much worse if you left for real."

I gave him a look. "Is that a compliment?"

Darrell seemed to think about that. "Probably. I am known to give them. Plus, no time passes while you're back there, spying on dead people. You just sort of zonk out, and then—bingo—you're all Becca again."

Wade listened to the whole thing and nodded. Just once. Slightly.

If it weren't so scary, it would be slightly ridiculous. I sat up in my seat, tried to smile. "Yeah, I'm a spy, all right. A spy in the house of the dead."

"Well, I'm calling your parents," Roald insisted, tugging out his cell phone.

I put my hand up. "Please don't. If they manage to get on tonight's flight from Austin, they'll be here tomorrow morning anyway. Maybe we should just follow what I see."

Roald continued to frown at me, but Darrell nodded. "You know, we probably should," he said. "Galina has Serpens, which means she'll steal this amber relic before we get near it."

"Actually, that's not right," I said as the driver continued to our safe flat on Chenies Mews in the Bloomsbury neighborhood. "Nicolaus told me that Serpens doesn't lead to this relic. It kills me that I was so close to this thing when we need it so bad. But I guess it had to be given to its first Guardian first. Still, we might have enough to follow the relic through history. Nicolaus gave me some clues. Maybe that's all we need. I mean, these visions should be good for something."

Wade was staring at me. It was an odd look. Then he said, "Your . . . nose."

I pushed my finger against my right nostril. "Sorry." It was only another drop. But it scared me. "All the excitement. I think I can remember the codes. Really."

They nodded quietly. As usual, you can't keep Lily quiet very long.

"Okay, but no splitting up," she said. "Not for a second. You start to get sucked back into five hundred years ago, you beep that alarm, baby—"

"I will." I tried to smile. "I really should write down

everything I remember before I don't remember it anymore."

"I'll remind you to remember not to forget to remember," said Darrell, being silly. The tension in the car was thick, and he's always good for breaking it up.

"Remember what?" I said. They laughed, all except Sara and Roald.

As we drove from street to street, I wrote furiously in my notebook. At the same time, Lily was busy on her tablet, trying to identify the house I saw, while Roald and Sara batted historical names back and forth.

"I just texted my dad," said Julian. "He doesn't know offhand what officials drive cars without plates, but we'll find out. Dad has friends in important places. In the meantime, we should keep off the main avenues."

The driver gave a nod, slowed, and wove through a series of narrow streets.

After a while Roald said, "Sara and I are pretty much agreed that according to what you told us, Becca, the Guardian you saw is Saint Thomas More. He was a politician and writer in the sixteenth century. Only we think he lived in Chelsea on the other side of London, and not near where you saw him."

I stopped writing.

Lily raised her hand. She had a page up on her tablet. "He *did* live in Chelsea, but that was later. In 1517, he lived in Bucklersbury Passage. *And* he had a daughter named Meg who was about twelve then. *And* Meg had a younger sister named Elizabeth. Thomas also supported the Charterhouse hospital and took in orphans, like the girl Joan who couldn't talk. He sounds like a pretty decent guy."

"And the book he had just written?" I said. "The one with codes? I'm trying to remember the code Nicolaus wrote for Meg before I look in the diary. I don't want to get confused. There's so much he told me."

"I don't know about the codes," Sara said, "but he may have been talking about Thomas's book called *Utopia*. It's his most well-known work."

"It came out in 1516," said Lily, reading her tablet. "You said it was recent."

"More was powerful during the reign of Henry the Eighth," Roald said.

"Henry had six wives," said Lily. "Not at the same time, of course."

Roald nodded. "Henry sentenced Thomas More to death."

"Not his head," said Darrell. "It was his head, right? Henry chopped it off."

"Not him personally," said Wade. "Kings have special guys for that."

"That's some kind of job, isn't it?" said Darrell. "How

44

do you practice? With watermelons?"

Lily cupped her hand over her mouth. "Gross, you guys."

"Boys, not funny," said Sara. "Death is death."

"So, we're right," I said. "It sounds like it was Thomas More. Copernicus knew what would happen, but he couldn't tell Thomas. People who traveled in time, he said, were like blind men with torches."

When I looked up from my notebook, Wade was staring at me again. It wasn't at my nose this time, but he looked as if he had something to say.

"You don't believe me, do you?" I asked him.

He blinked, then shook his head. "I just think we need to get back to the safe flat. Becca, you're kind of pale. Like falling-down-unconscious pale."

Lily gasped. "Excuse me, Wade? You *never* tell someone, and by *someone* I mean us"—she pointed to herself and me—"that we don't look good. It's rude."

Wade frowned. "Well, I didn't mean it that way—"

"Oh, so you think Becca looks good?" asked Darrell.

"That's not what I meant!"

"So you think she's ugly?" said Lily.

"Guys, give it a break," Sara said. "We could all use a rest—"

"And food!" said Darrell. "I'm sure I speak for everyone when I say we need food. And if I *don't* speak for

45

everyone, it's because you're wrong. To put it another way—food now. Food now!"

Julian laughed. "I know just the place."

"But before food, I need that book," I said. "Unless I'm a total lunatic, and I may be, Copernicus gave me major clues about where to find the relic. I need to get a copy of *Utopia*. If what I remember translates to real words, maybe that will prove it once and for all." I looked right at Wade. "To everybody."

"Hey, I didn't say I didn't—"

"Book now!" said Darrell. "Then food now!"

"The closest bookshop is twelve minutes away," said Lily, looking up from her tablet. She showed Julian what she'd found.

"I know it," he said. "Driver, please take us to Lamb's Conduit."

Darrell made a face. "I really hope that's a street and not a body part."

CHAPTER SEVEN

Halfway up Lamb's Conduit, a cool street with parquet-style paving bricks, was Pucker's Books, a teeny shop shoehorned between a sparkling new Pret A Manger restaurant and a bustling bicycle repair.

The limo eased down the block and around a corner to the nearest parking spot. We got out and studied the street. No black cars. No motorcycles. No Hatman.

Julian said, "You know what—you go in. We stumbled upon Markus Wolff and the black car, but I want to make sure we're not being tracked. I'm going to upgrade the software on your phones remotely from the servers at the Ackroyd Foundation in Fleet Street. I'll snag a cab. The limo will stay. I'll be right back."

"Sounds good," said Roald. "We'll eat at Pret A

Manger when we're done."

Julian gave us a nod, looked both ways, and jogged away.

The moment I pushed open the front door of Pucker's and a bell chimed, the aroma of dry paper overpowered me—tens of thousands of freshly printed and antique books were crammed onto wooden shelves, in teetering stacks on the floor, in skyscraper piles on old oak tables. They were jammed into the window seats, across the aisles, on the stairs leading up, on the stairs leading down, and on every available inch of the cashier's counter.

No wonder the little old guy behind the register was busy coughing his head off. "Wel"—gasp—"come," he said, raising his reading glasses to reveal the largest eyes I'd ever seen. "How can I—*kakk*—help you?"

Roald kept his arms firmly around Sara's shoulders until he settled her on a small bench made of encyclopedias. "We're interested in Thomas More."

"Ah, the More the—*ggg*—merrier!" The proprietor gagged, waiting for our reaction. I smiled. Apparently, not enough for him.

"So," he said sharply, "which do you want? The saint—*kkk*—the scholar, the martyr, or the—*ggg*—writer? We have the complete works, quite a steal at—*gkk-kk*—four hundred pounds."

48

"We'd like something light enough to carry around," said Lily with a smile.

The man narrowed his large eyes at her. "American humor. Well, then his *selected* works—*ggg-kkkk!*—are available. In p-p-paperback. Would you like new or used?"

"Either," I said.

"Buying a used book doesn't *g-g-g-k-kive* its author any royalties," the man said, holding his fingers tight on the bridge of his nose.

"Then new."

He pointed a slender finger at a teetering shelf at eye level across the room. "Over there. And Thomas More, dead as he is, thanks you for his sixpence."

"Is that a lot?" asked Darrell.

"No."

I scooted straight for the shelves—or I would have if stacks of old travel and art magazines hadn't blocked my way—and before long located a new paperback copy of *Utopia*. As I picked my way back to the others, I read the back cover and discovered that the book was a fictional account of the island of Utopia, a perfect society that wasn't so perfect after all. "It sounds like the book Thomas More was telling Nicolaus about."

"I love that," said Lily. "You and Nick on a first-name basis."

"Eh?" said the proprietor. "Nicolaus? Nicolaus Kratzer?"

I spun around. "Kratzer? I know that name!"

"Kratzer was the king's astronomer," the man said. "He knew Thomas More, of course, taught his children."

I turned to Wade and mouthed *I know!* then grinned.

"Does the book have the code you saw?" Sara whispered.

I flipped past the book's introduction, and there it was, right at the beginning.

A   Ö
B   ⊖
C   ⦶
D   ⊙
E   ◯
F   ⊙
G   ⊃
H   ⊂
I   ◠
K   ◡
L   ⊖
M   △
N   ⌐
O   ∟

P ⌐

Q ⌐

R □

S ⊟

T ⊞

V ⊡

X ⊟

Y ⊡

"I need this book. I have to have it," I said.

"Oh, Becca, I hope it works," said Sara.

"It will," said Lily. "This is Becca we're talking about."

Using the Ackroyd credit card, we bought *Utopia* and a copy of More's *Selected Writings* that Darrell found in the English history section, which happily included a bio written by More's son-in-law William Roper, who eventually married Meg, which was fun to know. It also had some of Thomas's letters.

After paying the sneezing guy, we ducked out and slipped into the Pret A Manger next door and pushed two tables together. I got an egg sandwich and a bottle of water and set them on the table to block Copernicus's diary from view. It was covered in a now-tattered copy of the London *Times*, but was still strange enough to draw attention if people saw it too closely. I put *Utopia* and my notebook next to it.

"Thomas More made up an alphabet for the people on his fictional island of Utopia," I said. "It's basically a substitution code of"—I counted—"twenty-two characters, which means that it probably translates to Latin, with some of the characters serving as two letters, like *I* for *J* or *V* for *U* and no *Z*."

I didn't want to read the words Copernicus had written for me in the diary before I remembered the four words he had written for Meg. Because of all the other junk zooming around my head, however, I was pretty astonished that the words were actually still there, as if waiting for me.

ΦΌGⅢ□ ⅭLⅢLⅭLϽⴱΔ
LΦ⊟ⴱL⊟ ΦⴲⅢⅭÓⴲΌⴲ

I translated the symbols into letters. The code did turn out to be in Latin.

"The first of Elizabeth's words is *caestv*, the second is *horologivm*, which, after you change each *v* to a *u*, are Latin for 'glove' and 'clock.' Meg's words are *ocvlos* or *oculos*, which means 'eyes,' and *citharae*, which means 'lutes.'"

"What did he mean by giving each daughter different words?" asked Wade.

I tried to read a tone into his question but couldn't. "I don't know yet. It has to do with a portrait of them."

"*Glove, clock, eyes,* and *lutes,*" said Lily, "There aren't any clocks or gloves in the constellations, are there?"

"No," said Roald, "but dozens of eyes. Wade, your star chart can help."

We had learned from searching for other relics that each was named after a constellation usually seen in the sky over where the relic was hidden. Wade carefully spread his star map on the table and began hunting.

"This reminds me of when we started our search for Serpens at the Morgan in New York," said Lily. "We figured out that mystery. We'll get this one, too."

"By the way, the painter who painted Thomas More and his family," Darrell said, "is a German. Hans Holbein. It was in 1527. Ten years later, like Nick said."

Roald sat forward over his coffee. "What really interests me is the business of the damage Copernicus thought he did. Had he seen what the Order would do if they had the astrolabe? Or what he himself did? And what kind of horrors could a good person really do if he wasn't forced to?"

"He told me that 'because she lives . . . there is the evil,'" I said, "but not who or what he meant. He held back from me. I don't know why."

"Okay, if we set aside the clock and eye business,"

said Darrell, "there's still the code he wrote in his diary. What does that mean?"

I turned the diary pages until I found what he'd written as a clue for us.

○⊡L △L⊡⊞⋻○ ⊟△⊖○◇○ ⊞⊟⊡⊡○△

It took me a few minutes to work out the translation, which I copied into my notebook. *"Dvo mortvi vmbrae tvrrem.* In other words, *Duo mortui umbrae turrem.* 'Two dead' . . . something. He said it would happen 'after nightfall tonight.' He didn't say whose nightfall."

Lily keyed the words into the translation program. *"Duo* and all that means 'two dead in the tower's shadow,' or 'in the shadow of the tower.' *Umbrae* means 'shadows.' *Turrem* means 'tower.'"

Two dead in the shadow of the tower. I didn't like how it sounded, but my brain was blurring out on me. The pieces weren't fitting. Not yet.

"Two dead in the shadow of the tower," Wade repeated under his breath. "The Tower of London? That's where Thomas was executed. Him and another guy?"

"Probably by that professional executioner," said Darrell.

"Don't start that again," said Lily.

"Well, I just hope the relic is still around," said Sara. "The archives in Austin have diaries about the great London fire. Hundreds of buildings were burned to the ground. And in 1940 and '41, German air raids bombed much of the city."

Roald looked up from his sandwich. "To me, the fact that Galina is so obsessed with the hunt, and has sent her personal archaeologist here, must mean that she thinks a relic is still around. We should presume that, too."

His phone rang. He answered it. He didn't put it on speaker, but he didn't leave the table, either. We listened to bits and pieces of his conversation with someone he apparently hadn't expected to call him, though who aside from Terence and Julian had the number, I couldn't guess. Finally, Roald left the table, still talking, and I saw my face in the window. Wade was right. My skin was pasty, my hair a mess from the rain.

I was about to run off to the bathroom when Lily pushed a napkin at me.

"Here. Eww."

"What?"

I put my finger under my nostril. Another nosebleed. "Sorry! Uck." I daubed the napkin under my nose. More than a drop this time. I covered it pretty well, but all I could think of was Helmut Bern and *his* bloody nose.

"Maybe we should get you checked out by a doctor," Sara said quietly.

"Or at least back to the safe flat so you can rest," Lily said.

"What about the amber thing?" said Darrell. "Don't we have to follow the clues—clock and glove and eye and the dead guys at the Tower of London?"

"Once we take care of Becca, sure," said Lily. "A doctor, a nice rest . . ."

"Hey, I'm not an invalid," I said. "It's a bloody nose, not cancer." Which was a harsh thing to say, but it stopped everyone from going on and on. "I'm okay."

Roald came back to the table, off the phone now. "Listen. I, or we, have been invited to chat with a former instructor of mine. Felix Ross was a visiting professor in Berlin. He's a crack physicist. Time travel was his thing, as I recall. Maybe we could get him to talk about some of our different theories."

"Dad, this is great," said Wade, folding up his star chart. "We could use some input. He might tell us what we all need to know."

When he said *we all*, he was looking exactly *not* at me.

"Hold on, suspicion taking over," said Lily, tapping into her tablet. "Felix Ross, huh? And how did he happen to get your cell number?"

"Ah," said Roald. "When I asked him about that

he laughed and said he could tell me, just not over the phone. He can see us anytime."

Sara turned to me. "Becca, we can still see a doctor. I think we should."

"Thanks," I said. "But I'm good. Let's keep moving."

I think I upset Sara when I said *cancer*. After all, wasn't radium poisoning what we suspected Andreas Copernicus had died of? Could Bern be showing the same symptoms? Could I? I stuffed a few napkins into my jacket pocket, hoping I wouldn't need more than that.

Lily's online search found an answer. "Felix Ross teaches the history of science in the Department of Physics and Astronomy at University College London. Plus, he's *Sir* Felix now. He's been knighted."

Darrell shared a look with Wade. "Is being an English knight different from being a Teutonic knight?"

"Yeah," said Wade, "you get to have six wives."

Lily winced. "Uck, both of you."

The doors of the restaurant swung open and Julian stepped inside. His cheeks were red. He had been running. He pressed his hand low—*stay down*—and turned to look at the street, then came to our table and crouched down beside it.

"Stay seated for a moment, then go out the back," he said.

57

At that moment our limo drove quickly down the street outside, followed by the black BMW, whose windows were open. Even crouching, I saw two men in the front, and the back was full, too. The driver sped up after the limo. Pedestrians jumped back to the sidewalks; then came a sudden thudding sound.

"Someone's shooting!" a woman called out from a table. "Someone's—"

More shots from down the street. "Now," said Julian. "Everybody out."

I stuffed a few more napkins into my pocket and slung my bag over my shoulder. We scurried with the other patrons out the back. From there we hurried across backyards and lots and finally into a street called Barbon Close.

Julian drew us near one of the houses. "We don't know about the car yet. Maybe it was just cruising and spotted our limo. We can't find Markus Wolff, either, but my dad discovered that your Umbrella Man is named Archibald Doyle. He's a seedy character who's likely a part of this surveillance."

When we told him we were heading to University College London, he said, "That should be safe enough. Lots of people there. I'll check in with Dad and meet up with you later."

"Becca, are you up for this?" Sara asked.

I was tired and I ached all over, but I needed to hear from a time-travel expert. Besides, after our little sit-down at Pret A Manger, I felt more like myself. Calmer. More in control.

"I am if you are," I said.

Sara nodded firmly. "I am."

We followed Julian up to the next street, Great Ormond Street, where the famous children's hospital was. We split up there, but not before I read the sign on the front of the building we huddled next to: Children with Cancer.

As we hurried off, I shivered all over again.

CHAPTER EIGHT

We doglegged through the streets to University College, a cluster of brick, stone, and glass structures from the nineteenth and twentieth centuries, with courtyards and walkways connecting them. Ten minutes later, we were on the third floor of the sciences building, in Sir Felix Ross's spacious office.

He was tall and slender and beamed a great big smile at us from under his gray mustache. "Yes! Why, yes!" he said brightly, as if in answer to a question. He shook Roald's hand firmly and gave Sara a peck on the cheek. "So good, so very good to see you, Roald and Sara, and children. Come in. Come in!"

He waved his hand at a cluster of leather chairs surrounding a big oak desk. His gray hair was longish and brushed back over his ears. He wore a bulky brown sport coat, brown pants, and scuffed brown shoes. "Please do sit yourselves down." His voice was crisp and formal, but as soft and leathery as the old chairs.

While Roald introduced us all, I looked around. Sir Felix's office was like the inside of a well-worn box, paneled from the floor to the ceiling with aged wood and shelving, and it smelled of the past mingled with what I guessed was old pipe smoke. Behind the desk were three old astronomical prints in frames. A large book—in German—was open on his desk as though he'd just been reading it. I remembered Lily saying he taught the history of science.

"Well, well . . ." He slouched into his desk chair, biting between his lips an unlit pipe, which bobbed up and down with each word. "Well, well. First let me say that I am utterly delighted you could make it today. And so sorry to hear of old Professor Vogel's sad demise. You were close, I take it?"

"Very, thanks. It was quite a shock," Roald said.

"He was Uncle Henry to me," said Wade.

"Was he? Well, I am sorry. A tragedy. Not an accident, I hear. Dreadful."

We all felt a pang in our chests then, I think. Wade and Roald sure did.

"Now," Sir Felix said. "Tell me all that you've been

up to, Professor Kaplan!"

Roald smiled. "Well, I think we're interested first of all in how you got my cell number. As it is, not many people actually know we're in London."

Sir Felix laughed around his still-unlit pipe. "Oh that! It's rather hush-hush, but I happen to have a little working relationship with MI5, the domestic intelligence service. I explain nuclear science to them; they tell me odds and ends of this and that. Your name was in a list of physicists in Britain. Don't ask me how they got wind of you, but they did."

Sara raised her eyebrows. "That is interesting," she said.

"And lucky for me, no?" Sir Felix said with another laugh. "Now, tell all!"

After a bit of catch-up and chat about what he was doing professionally, Roald got to it. Or tried to get to it. He started with a few words, and I realized it was almost impossible to talk about without sounding crazy.

"Out with it, old boy!" Sir Felix chuckled.

"All right," Roald said. "Sir Felix, what do you know about . . . it sounds ridiculous, of course, but . . . time, the science of time?"

"The science of time!" he said, drawing a long breath between his clamped teeth. "The science of time. Well, time can be said to go back some six thousand years if you take the view of some biblical scholars. Or thirteen-point-eight billion years, if you allow for the Big Bang notion. Now, if you ask me . . ."

Roald shook his head, more uncomfortable than before. "Excuse me, Sir Felix, I should have been more specific. I meant more the idea of *traveling* . . ."

"Traveling? You mean like from London to Liverpool?"

"I mean like from London to Londinium."

"To Londinium . . . ?" He frowned, removed his pipe from his mouth, and stared at Roald. "Londinium . . . ah. Time travel!" He laughed without taking his eyes off Roald. "I take it you're serious? As in practical travel forward and backward in time. Not the silly popular culture and whatnot. Well, well."

Roald glanced at Sara as if for help when Wade jumped in. "I mean, we know that time machines don't exist, of course. But the theories about time travel?"

"Exactly . . . ," Sara agreed. She was holding my hand in hers.

"Well, then. Well, then." Sir Felix stood up now. He was silhouetted against the window, as slender and tall as a reed. The sun was now beating away the last lingering clouds. I glanced at the old clock on the wall over the door.

It was nearing twelve fifteen.

"To me, the most *workable* theory is that time is like a *river*. A river of thick, almost unmoving fluid. I rather like the term *cosmic molasses*. Normally, we only travel forward on this river. However, if the conditions are proper, if the stars, as they say, are aligned and one can produce a powerful enough jolt of energy—nuclear energy, I should think—there *is* a theoretical possibility of pushing or drilling against the current."

My heart beat faster. I felt a little light-headed, but I also sensed that we were finally getting somewhere. Apparently, I didn't look great. Sir Felix startled me.

"My dear, you look faint. Come over here, please." And he took my bag and set it on the desk, and pulled his own chair out. He guided me around to it and sat me down. "There you are. Lean back. This will make you feel better. You look like you've been through it a bit. Shall I order some tea, dear?"

"I'm all right," I said, checking my nose. It was dry. "No tea. But thank you."

He smiled like a grandfather. "Now, then . . . oh yes. When you do force your way back—by whatever mechanism—you create a wake. A disturbance in the force, as they say. Actually, it's a sort of trench or tunnel in the fluid of time." He paused to let that settle in. "Some Renaissance theorists called it a sort of hole."

A hole. Copernicus had used the same words in his

diary and even said them when I'd seen him earlier. A hole. *A hole in the sky.*

"Oh, a tiny hole, mind you," Sir Felix went on. "Experimental physicists today call it a microhole. A whorl in the air that circles about the path connecting one temporal location with another. The problem is that going to the past is like breaking into a locked room. Once you open that door, things can enter and leave that should not. Terrible mess." He bit his pipe. "Of course, no one's done it."

I shivered. "You said nuclear energy might be needed?"

"Oh, rather," Sir Felix said. "To create a hole of any duration would require a tremendous blast. Pinpointed to a direct spot, I would imagine."

Somehow, Kronos had done that to me. It had zapped me just enough to cook a part of my brain. I "went back," but only mentally, not physically.

Sir Felix paced across the brightening window and stopped. "Why do you want to know about such a specific event, if I may ask?"

There was an uncomfortable silence. I expected Sara or Roald to make some kind of polite answer, but Darrell saved it by going in another direction.

"A black car followed us this morning. We think they were spies."

Sir Felix seemed taken aback for a moment, then he set his pipe on the desk. "A black car, you say? Is that unusual? We do have black cars in London."

"This one didn't have any license plates," Lily added.

"Oh," he said. "Oh, dear. I *have* heard of that. A mystery. Or perhaps nothing of the sort. Look, I'll ask one or two of my spy chaps to check it out and get back to you. You know what, better idea. Roald, you and I can talk to them together." He checked his watch. "What do you say to that?"

"Thank you, Sir Felix," Roald said, relaxing visibly. "That would help."

"Splendid," he said, taking up his pipe again. "I *do* carry some weight as a knight of the empire. Come, then, let's do it right away. And the rest of you, well, you're obviously working on some fascinating little story here, so while Roald and I do some hush-hush work, let me suggest you chat with my best research chap. Simon Tingle has what you might call an eidetic memory. A walking database of the odd facts, he is. He's down one level, in the lab. I'll tell him you're coming. Ask him anything. I like to put my people through their paces! Here is your bag, Becca. I hope you're feeling better."

"Yes, thank you. I am."

"Splendid. Roald, come with me. Ta-ta!"

CHAPTER NINE

Sir Felix showed us to the elevator and took Roald by the elbow and went off with him, reminiscing all the way. We went down one floor to the lab.

We found Simon Tingle in a windowless office, lying nearly supine in a desk chair, his feet up, head back, eyes closed, and mumbling to himself. "Divorced, *executed*, died, divorced, *executed*, widowed—"

"The six wives of Henry the Eighth!" Lily exclaimed. "I know about them!"

Simon Tingle jumped up from his chair. "Exactly right! Wait, who are *you*?" In jumping up, however, he knocked over a cup and saucer, spilling milky tea all over his desk. "Oh dear. Now *look* what I've made myself do! I'm so sorry, *so* sorry! Simon Tingle here. How can you help me? That is, how can *I* help *you*?"

"Excuse us," Sara said. "Sir Felix invited us to come and see you . . ."

"He said you could help us look up some information," said Wade.

"Look up! No, no! I never look *up*," the man said as he soaked up the spilled tea with the sleeve of his jacket. "Look *into*, yes. *Into*. You see, it's all in here." He tapped the side of his head several times with a finger dripping with tea. "In *here*." He licked his finger. "You see, they call me Mr. Memory, you see."

Again I didn't see, but Sara said it was from a movie. "Mr. Memory was a spy who smuggled secrets by committing them to memory."

The man's whole round face lit up. "You are *correct*, madam! *The Thirty-Nine Steps*. Famous British thriller film directed by Alfred Hitchcock in 1935 and *loosely* based on the 1915 novel by adventure writer John Buchan. *Loosely* based, I say"—his voice went down a register—"because the *film* actually *creates* the character of Mr. Memory, a fellow *not* in the original novel, but a clever *fabrication*."

"Wow, you're a walking Wikipedia!" said Lily.

"Pishposh!" he snarled happily. "Far better. I am *one hundred percent* accurate." Then his deep blue eyes twinkled with excitement and he rubbed his hands together.

"But Sir Felix told you I can *answer* your questions, and answer them I *shall*! Begin the inquisition!"

Simon shut his eyes and perched his fingers on his temples, while we told him what we knew about Thomas More. It wasn't much, but he instantly took over, describing More's life—and death—in exhaustive detail, ending with, "There *is* a famous family portrait. It is a *copy* dating from 1592 of an *earlier* 1527 painting by the German artist *Hans Holbein*, which has unfortunately been *lost*, although the later copy was most certainly rendered from Holbein's original."

Wade and I both wrote this down in our notebooks.

"The portrait is a *lovely* piece of work now at Nostell Priory in West Yorkshire," Simon continued. "As I cannot open my *brain* to show you the portrait as it exists up *here*"—more head tapping—"I will require the use of what is termed a *book*. Move not." He twirled on his heels and exited the room. Less than three minutes later, he stormed back in. He opened a huge book on his desk, spilling the rest of his tea—"Oh, Simon!"—and showed us a large portrait.

"Here, you *see*," he said, and ran his finger over a group of six men, six women, two dogs, and a monkey inside a house that looked nothing like the Old Barge. "The seated gentleman directly in the center is Sir Thomas *More*. Position matters in Holbein. His art is

69

full of *codes*, you see. More's *father* is the older gentleman sitting next to him. This is More's house at *Chelsea*."

Thomas was dressed in a heavy black robe with sleeves of crimson, a large gold chain around his neck, while his father was in bright red, trimmed in white. The women were mostly in long black dresses with white bodices, and formal bonnets of black and white with gold trim.

"On the far right is More's second wife, two of his daughters, his household staff. Holbein couldn't resist symbols in his portraits, and this image is no exception. Notice the monkey, the lutes, this little brown-and-white dog curled asleep on the floor. Everything means something."

The lutes. The sleeping dog!

"Is this woman pulling on her glove by any chance Elizabeth?" I asked, pointing to a young woman who stood just to the left of the sleeping dog.

"Right you are!" Simon said with a broad smile. "And this, sitting second from the right, is *Margaret*—called Meg—Thomas's favorite. Terrible about More, of course. He lost his head some eight years after this grouping."

"Might we have a few moments alone with the picture?" Sara asked.

"Why I . . . yes, of course! I do need to brew another cup of *tea*, don't I? I surely *do*!" He laughed and stormed out of the room as he had just stormed into it.

In the quiet I studied the picture, but my heart wasn't quiet. I felt as if I'd stuck my finger into an electrical socket and current was zapping through me.

"I know these people," I said, riveted on their faces. "Or younger versions of them. They were at the house in Bucklersbury, but everything is here that Copernicus said. Elizabeth has got a glove half on her right hand. There's a clock over Thomas's head. There are a couple of lutes and lots of eyes. It's all here. Meg remembered everything Copernicus told her."

"He must have seen the painting later," said Wade. "Through his microhole."

"Okay, but what do we do with all this information?" said Darrell. "Are we supposed to connect the words to each daughter?"

"Connect the words?" I said.

"Draw a line," he said, leaning over the picture. "Meg's words were *eyes* and *lutes*, right? So go from her eyes to the lutes."

"Yes, and for Elizabeth, go from her glove to the clock," Lily added. "Maybe they form a letter or a shape."

Wade nodded slowly. "Good. I like that."

"Thank you for approving of our idea." Lily ran her fingertip from Elizabeth's glove to the clock over Thomas's head, and another from Margaret's eyes to the lutes behind Elizabeth, continuing the line until the lines intersected.

"Whoa, a kind of tilted *X*," Darrell said. "What does *that* mean?"

"Not an *X*," said Wade, quickly tugging out his star chart. "Not an *X*. It's a cross. Look here. Becca, you said that Copernicus told Thomas to keep the 'two equal arms' of the amber relic separate. To me, two equal arms form a cross. And look, the tilted angle of the two lines intersecting in the painting is the same angle in the constellation called Crux. The relic Copernicus gave Thomas is Crux."

If it seemed easy, it was, but only because for the last few weeks the four of us—and Sara and Roald, too—had been training our minds to solve riddles. To decrypt codes and follow mysteries. Every clue had been left specifically to point to a relic. Not for the Order to find. Not for Galina to steal. But for the Guardians to know about and protect. Riddles and puzzles were necessary to keep the relics hidden—but also to make them findable. Nicolaus had intended that, too.

"Let's get back to the painting," said Darrell. "Are we saying that Copernicus told Meg to tell Holbein about the clock and the eye so that he would paint them into his painting for Guardians like us to find?"

A smile was growing on Wade's face. "I think that's

exactly it. Copernicus traveled back and forth in time. Sir Felix told us about the hole in time. Copernicus described a hole in the sky. Whatever you call it, his astrolabe was able to go through it, and he was able to hide clues in different times."

"That could very easily lead to trouble," said Sara.

"The horror of knowing, right, Bec?" Lily added. "Nicolaus told you that."

He did tell me that. He also told me that because she lives, there is "the evil." I didn't really understand how much horror there would be until later.

After nightfall.

Which, when I checked the clock in Simon's office, was getting closer every minute. Would there be enough time to solve the riddle? I didn't know, but I was beginning to understand what Nicolaus meant by the *horror of knowing and not being able to warn*.

CHAPTER TEN

Simon rushed back in, barely keeping his new cup of tea upright. "Must run," he said. "Sir Felix needs me pronto. Here's my number, in case you need anything else." He scribbled it on a scrap of paper and thrust it in my hand. "Now, pardon my rudeness, but I mustn't keep the master waiting!"

We said our quick good-byes to him and met Roald in the lobby. He told us he described the BMW on the phone to Sir Felix's chums in MI5 and seemed convinced that they would soon be able to identify the car.

Even though the university was very close to our safe flat in Chenies Mews, once out on the street we wound our way to it in the usual crazy way.

"Don't take the highway; take the spy way," Darrell

quipped as we walked a wiggly maze of streets until we found ourselves finally between the walls of our own narrow passage. It was now a little after one o'clock. The roar of London was hushed in Chenies Mews, as if a blanket had been lowered over us.

Lily nudged me. "Safe," she said.

"Safe," I repeated, "but I'm so zonked, I'm claiming the first flat space I see. In fact, I'm probably already asleep. No, I *am* asleep. Listen. Zzzzzz . . ."

She laughed, her first laugh in a while. It was a warm laugh, and it warmed me, too, a little. I think she was relieved that I was acting normal, or at least trying. I guess I no longer seemed like a spy in the house of the dead.

Roald approached the door, then paused, holding his hand up. He looked around and even up over the rooftops behind us. Earlier, Darrell had suggested that if we didn't see anyone, there could still be drones watching us.

"I think we can all rest now," Roald said in a fatherly way as he slid the key and a plastic key card into the lock.

Seeing no one, we went in through the door and closed it. Roald keyed in an alarm code, then Sara pushed the lift button to bring us up to the flat, where there was a second door. We entered and reset that alarm, too.

What I really liked was that from the street our building looked more like a warehouse, and a slightly run-down one, at that. But inside the flat, it was homey and quietly luxurious.

"Terence and Julian sure know how to live," Darrell said as he plopped down on a long, overstuffed sofa in the main room. Wade settled across from him. There was a giant flat-screen TV on the wall opposite the large tinted window.

Roald walked through the rooms one after the other. When he returned to the main room, he smiled. "I've said this before, but Terence's flat really is perfect. The neighborhood is as quiet as a village, but it's right in central London. We have a view of both ends of the street and the alley behind us. We can relax."

"I've already started," said Darrell. "I had to. My legs told me to. They're asleep even as we speak."

Lily frowned at me over the dining room table. "You need sleep, too, missy. Not just your legs, but all of you."

"Becca, yes," said Sara, coming over and resting her hands on my shoulders. "You have to take care of yourself, or you'll be no good for whatever happens next."

Whatever happens next. *After nightfall.*

"I know." I was washed out, limp, sad, trying to slow my thumping pulse, trying to keep the next blackout at bay. "But there's work to do, too."

"We'll keep poring over this stuff," said Wade, making a show of being all alert and not tired at all. "We'll wake you for supper."

"Or if I discover the relic?" said Darrell.

"Either way is good," I said. "I just want one of the books." I kept the copy of *Selected Writings* and left *Utopia* on the table. "I'll probably fall asleep before I get anywhere."

"Before you do, tell us that you got to our room safely," Lily said. "Use your alarm if you don't make it."

"Deal. Good night. Even though it's afternoon."

"It's night somewhere," said Darrell. "Hong Kong, I think. Or China."

I gave a little wave to everyone and left them studying the clues we had so far. The Holbein portrait, which Lily found online, *Utopia*, what Simon had told us, Wade's star chart. We were pretty sure the relic was Crux and that its first Guardian had been Thomas More. If we followed that knowledge with the right connections, we could find it. Maybe. If it still existed.

I climbed four steps to the upper level and entered the backmost of the flat's four bedrooms, the one Lily and I shared.

"Did you make it to your room?" Lily called. "I didn't hear you beep."

"Because I made it!"

"Thank you!"

It wasn't my first time in that bedroom. We'd spent not only the last few days in that flat, but before that, too, when we were waiting to travel to Russia to search for Sara and Serpens. I liked it. A nightstand, two lamps, a bookcase, a desk, twin beds, each piled thickly with blankets and bedspreads that whispered to me to rest . . . to sleep.

And yet . . . I couldn't sleep. I needed to think. To understand what exactly had happened to me at Greywolf in Russia. *Kronos. It's all because of Kronos.*

Before anything, I went to the window, opened it a crack to let air in, then slipped off my shoes and lay on the bed. It was now about one thirty.

I set the book in my lap and looked at the picture on the cover. An engraving of More based on one of Holbein's many sketches. Thomas's eyes were riveting, kind but fierce. Closing mine, I conjured him, the imprisoned man, condemned to die a horrible death. I knew his fatherly face, his kind manner, his presence. I imagined him in his cell, tramping slowly back and forth across the stone floor, thinking about his family, about Meg. Then I thought of Roald, and of my father—how tortured they would be if they had to leave their loved ones behind.

Then . . .

. . . I smelled damp stone, and I shivered. I tried to open my eyes but couldn't. Something heavy rippled over me. My blood froze in my veins. There was a flash of light. Not from the room. It was dark around me. A light, winking in and out.

And I was in the prison cell, gasping for breath.

He was there. The kneeling shape of the man I'd seen in Bucklersbury. His homespun robes had been replaced by a plain brown frock too long for him. He had cinched it around his waist. He rose to his feet, made the sign of the cross, and tramped from one side of his cell to another. It was dark. One candle only. Shadows wavered on the walls.

But I wasn't alone with Thomas.

Copernicus moved behind me and watched the man's sad march from wall to wall. "Rebecca. My time is nearly up. Neither of us is here with Thomas. It is early in the morning, the sixth of July in 1535. He awaits his execution."

My chest felt as if it were turning to water. I shook, steadied myself. I had enough of my wits about me to remember something. "Where is Helmut Bern? I thought because we both were zapped by Kronos, he had to be here for me to see this. Is he close by now?"

Nicolaus had tears in his eyes. "He is near, released today from the Charterhouse to view his patron's death.

But listen. These names may mean little to you—Yellow Turban, Smyrna, Uskok. Remember them. I caused them, or I may as well have." All this was whispered quickly, intensely, as if his time was indeed running out. "You must speak of these horrors, or the Order will win."

I was frozen to the spot, between the poor man soon to die and Nicolaus whispering in my ear words I didn't understand. *Smyrna? Uskok?*

"But you couldn't have caused them. You're a good man—"

"What they call the horror of Holodomor? I mourn the millions of deaths I made happen! I never went farther forward than that. I stopped there."

I had to remember the name. Holodomor. "How many journeys did you take?"

"Just the two." He suddenly sucked in a breath. "Rebecca, my time is nearly done. You will need this! It is from the artist—"

"We know. It's Holbein. And that the relic is Crux."

"Then look here." Nicolaus drew a sheet of paper from inside his cloak. On it was a circle with a swirl of geometric symbols and letters radiating out from its center. It appeared to be part of a code wheel. I tried to take it in, sear every nuance of the image into my memory.

"Holbein's puzzle will help us find Crux?" I asked.

Before he could answer, he faded away and was gone. And I was gone from him. Thomas vanished, too. So did the stone walls surrounding him. I was in my bedroom at the safe flat. My nose had bled more this time. It took me more than one napkin to stop it, while Nicolaus's strange words rolled around my mind.

Holodomor. Smyrna. Uskok. Yellow Turban. What did they mean?

Pressing a second napkin to my nose, I did what Lily would do and went straight to the internet, keying in the words Nicolaus had told me. Do that yourself, and you'll know what the words mean, too. They were all tragic, terrible events. Horrifying episodes in history with tens of thousands of deaths, millions in the case of Holodomor. Untold suffering. How could Nicolaus have *caused* them? They were from different times, spanning nearly two thousand years.

I caused them, or I may as well have. A time traveler is like a blind man with a torch, setting fire to everything he stumbles into.

And the other thing. *You must speak of these horrors, or the Order will win.*

My stomach convulsed. I rushed to the bathroom and knelt on the tiles in front of the toilet. I waited. Nothing. I washed my face. I couldn't process it—the blind man with a torch. Did he mean that I was blind like that? That I *would* be?

I splashed cold water on my face again, toweled off, then closed the curtains, darkening the room from the afternoon sun and muffling the sounds of the city even more. I needed to calm myself. To understand.

I opened the book of Thomas's writings and turned instinctively to his letters. I wanted to hear his voice again, quiet, intelligent.

His short last letter, written to Meg, was unbearably sad. Tears came to my eyes with every gentle word, as I imagined tears had come to him when he wrote them. It made me miss my own family, and I longed to see them as soon as possible. Certainly, I didn't know *all* about Thomas More, but he loved Meg, loved the mute girl Joan Aleyn who still lived with him, he had a son, who he loved, his old father, his whole big family.

As I read the letter, I heard him giving Meg his last instructions.

> . . . to my good daughter Cecily . . . I
> send her my blessing and to all her
> children and pray her to pray for me.
> I send her a handkerchief . . .
> . . . to my good daughter Joan Aleyn
> to give her I pray you some kind
> answer . . .

> *. . . I send now unto my good daughter*
> *Clement her algorism stone . . .*
> *. . . I pray you . . . recommend me to*
> *my good son John More. . . .*

But it was his last words to Meg that finally broke my heart.

> *Fare well my dear child and pray for*
> *me, and I shall for you and all your*
> *friends that we may merrily meet in*
> *heaven. . . .*

Tears ran down my cheeks. In my mind I saw Thomas as clearly as I just had. It was later that same morning, and I saw Thomas take final leave of his cell. I watched him drag himself through the passages, out the Tower gate, then up the long, slow hill to the scaffold. I climbed the steps with him. I stood next to him. Together we searched the astonished and silent crowd for his beloved Meg—

I sat up and opened my eyes. "What's an *algorism stone?*"

I went back to the letter. *I send now unto my good daughter Clement her algorism stone.* Clement. I knew it was the last name of one of his wards, all of whom he called his daughters. Searching the footnotes at the bottom of the page, I discovered that an algorism stone was "a slate for calculations or, in this case, for jotting down thoughts best kept from prying eyes."

It wasn't enough.

I found two sites that dealt with Thomas More. One said that algorism stones, or slates, were often kept in boxes that also held charcoal pencils, paper, and sometimes the rods and beads of an abacus, which you could use to add, subtract, multiply, and divide. The "stone" referred to the slate, yes, but what if More meant "algorism stone" as a kind of code to mean the box the slate was in.

Then it hit me.

"The box that Holbein built for him! Nicolaus told Thomas to have him make a box. This is the box! It's where he hid the amber cross!" I jumped from bed. "Thomas had Crux with him in the Tower. With his last letter he was passing it on to his family. And the strange Holbein puzzle will tell us where it is!"

I was about to tear the door open and shout what I'd discovered when a sudden movement between the curtains caught my eye. I pulled one gently aside and saw a car enter the mews with the slow, slinky motion of a jungle animal prowling in the shadows. It was a black car.

"Lily! Everyone!" I pressed my thumb on the key-chain alarm. It was loud.

"What's going on up there?" Lily called. "Is your nose bleeding again?"

The car nosed halfway around the corner. It had no plates. Through the open window I heard a quiet click, and its engine cut out. *No . . . no . . .*

"The black car!" I shouted. "Everybody! The black car!"

CHAPTER ELEVEN

Someone—Wade or Darrell, I couldn't tell whose voice it was—called sharply from the living room. I heard the slap of bare feet on the hardwood. Sara was suddenly in my room, tugging me from the window. "Don't let them see you."

"How do they know?" I said. "Our phones are good; Julian said they were."

"I don't know." Her hand was insistent. "Just move from the window."

I couldn't. Both rear doors of the car opened at the same time, spreading like raven wings. I expected the men we'd seen earlier. Instead three men in black jumpsuits and body armor climbed out. One reached back into the rear seat and pulled out something. An automatic rifle. He handed it to the other man and took one for himself; then both pulled ski masks over their faces.

Roald was running down the hall, his hand clasped around his phone, the screen bright. "Time to use the rear exit. Bring only what you need. Out. Now!"

I grabbed my bag, and we hurried down the back stairs into the walled courtyard behind the building. Sara moved slowly, coughing into her hand, stifling the noise as much as she could. From the street in front came a sharp crack. The front-door alarm rang for a few seconds, then stopped.

"They've broken in!" Lily whispered.

I clamped my bag tight under my arm. Nicolaus's diary was more important than ever. It was his way of communicating directly to us. Directly to me.

"We need to get out of London," Roald said, punching the screen of his phone as he hurried through the alley, holding it to his ear. "I'm trying Terence—"

"Come on, Bec." Wade ran with me. I felt like a shadow, half there, half with Thomas More and Copernicus, with Holbein . . .

Sun broke through and shone down the passage behind Gower Street. It was a little after two now, and warming up, but I shivered. My armpits were grossly wet. My vision narrowed, squeezing everything into a tunnel. I couldn't breathe.

"Sir Felix wasn't able to do anything," Darrell grumbled. "Some help he is—"

"Darrell, he's only one man," his mother said, leaning on him.

We squirreled through the passage. Darrell helped his mother, but the moment he took his hand from her, she stumbled. Lily caught her. I wondered how long it would take the men to realize we'd gone out the back. Sara was on the move again, holding herself together, steadier now. Roald, Lily, and Wade were first to reach the end of the passage. Wade squirmed ahead like the leader. He put his hand up for us to shush, peeked out, looked back at us, didn't move.

"Is someone out there?" Lily whispered.

Wade shook his head. "Becca, are you all right? Have you been crying?"

I was leaning against the wall, the last of us, even behind Sara. My face must have been deathly. "I went back again. This time, Nicolaus showed me a puzzle. Holbein made it, he said. It had German characters and symbols." My head pounded. I checked my nose. Dry for now. "Let's just get out of here!"

Still on the phone, Roald slipped by Wade and looked out. A window broke behind us, a harsh sound in the quiet of the alley. "Someone call Julian."

"I will. I'll tell him about the Holbein puzzle, too." Wade pushed his hand into his pocket, tugged out his phone, and hit the screen with his thumb. As he did, I hurriedly explained my theory about the algorism stone.

"I think it could be a code for the relic box," I said. "Thomas had it with him in the Tower of London, then gave it to his family—"

Another crash of glass behind us, then clipped shouting.

"Now." Roald slid out onto Gower Street. We followed one by one, me last.

Darrell scanned the traffic. "We can't use main streets—"

Julian's calm voice crackled through the speaker on Wade's phone. "I'm working on the car, but no luck yet. I just rechecked; your phones are good. Where are you now?"

"Top of Gower Street," Darrell said, still looking out between the buildings. "It's busy. I don't see anyone on this side of the flat, though. Not yet."

"Becca saw a puzzle," Wade said into his phone. "By Hans Holbein—"

"My dad needs to know that," Julian said.

Suddenly Terence was on Roald's phone, also on speaker. "Your Umbrella Man—Archie Doyle—is one slippery agent. He's already killed eight people for the

Order, including your friend Boris. He's lurking around, so be careful. In the meantime, run across the street and back to the university. There's no car access on that part of campus. Then go north—"

"North?" said Lily. "We're from Texas. Everything's north!"

"From Chenies Mews to Gower is east," Julian added from Wade's phone. It was a weird multiway conversation. "Go north to Euston Station. Listen, Dad, they found a German puzzle." We heard a door slam in the background.

"German puzzle, let me work on that," said Terence. "But look, you people want Euston train station, not the Underground. I suggest splitting up, at least for now. Sara, go to the third cashier and ask for 'five tickets for the next train to Bishops Stortford via the London Midland line.' Say it exactly that way. Roald, meet me at Autonoleggio Nazionale in forty minutes. Just you alone. I have information. Too much for the phone. Roald, forty minutes. Hurry!"

"I should know about the black car soon," said Julian. "Talk to you later."

They both signed off, and Roald's phone went silent.

"What Terence said sounded like Italian," said Darrell. "Is there a new code?"

"He's trying it out in his new novel," Roald said.

"Different languages mean different things. Italian means cut any numbers in half. He'll meet me in twenty minutes. Also, Bishops Stortford is where his mother was born. The third cashier will give you the proper destination."

"*Autonoleggio nazionale* means something like 'national rental car,'" I said.

After a few seconds on her tablet, Lily said, "There's National Car Hire on Pentonville Road. A twenty-minute walk. You'll just have time." She showed him the screen.

"Got it. Kids, Sara," said Roald, gathering us to him, "I'll draw them away. You help one another to the station. I'll join you after I meet with Terence."

"Wait!" Sara said fiercely, grasping his sleeve. "They're killers working with Markus Wolff. You don't know what they'll do. I mean, you *do* know what they'll do. I don't want to split up. We shouldn't—"

Roald nodded, holding her to him. "Doyle I don't know about, but Wolff seems like the senior man here. He'll wait until he gets a clear run at us—"

"All the more reason to stay with us, Uncle Roald," Lily said.

"All the more reason to throw them off," Roald said. "Look, I know what I'm doing. Julian and Terence will run interference. You have a lead. Follow it."

Roald kissed Sara quickly, then pushed for the last time through the narrow cut-through and was out on Gower Street, running south, which Lily said was exactly the wrong direction from Pentonville Road. I couldn't tell whether the BMW was in the crush of traffic, but if it was, it must have seen him. He zigzagged along the sidewalk, waving his arms, stopping, stepping out into the road, stepping back. It was quite a show. Sara groaned under her breath.

"All right," said Wade, taking the lead again. "We can do this."

We waited for a lull in the traffic, checked and rechecked both ways before crossing, then sprinted across Gower and into the busy university.

Students rushed across the lawns to get to classes; groups of faculty chatted, smoked. Mothers with strollers, joggers, young people tossing Frisbees, everyone going on with their normal lives.

We hurried diagonally across the yards, keeping ourselves as inconspicuous as possible. I kept my eyes open for Archie Doyle, but my mind was swimming with Thomas More's algorism stone and Copernicus's strange warning.

I'd have to tell everyone that, too. And soon.

Finally, we came out to the broad, frantic Euston Road. The pedestrian path across it to the train station was a zigzag over one lane, a median, and another lane. The instant the lights turned in our favor, we moved through the mass of bodies pouring out of the terminal and entered the station at last.

CHAPTER TWELVE

Like all the train stations we'd been in since the relic hunt started, Euston Station boomed with people and announcements and a million sights and smells and other distractions. On top of that, every face looked sinister.

"Mom, remember," Darrell said. "You ask the third cashier for 'five tickets for the next train to Bishops Stortford via the London Midland line.'"

"I remember, thanks. Go to that newsstand, all of you"—Sara pointed like Roald would do—"pick up a tourist guidebook, and stay put. Do. Not. Move. I'll be right back." She gave us a stern look, then headed off to the ticket line. She seemed small and frail in the crowd, but she moved quickly across the floor.

My head was spinning. I had to get the puzzle on paper before I forgot it. The room was so loud that I couldn't concentrate. Maybe I'd already forgotten it, the strange lines and symbols. Then, on the way to the newsstand, I froze.

Lily tugged at my bad arm. I winced, but I wouldn't budge.

"Wait," she said. "Are you seeing Henry the Eighth in your mind? Is he as fat as they say?"

"No," I said. "I mean, he might be; that's not it. Someone's here in the station."

"Wolff?" said Darrell, scanning the huge room. "Or Archie Doyle?"

"I don't know," I said. I sensed a presence. "If we're not being tracked electronically, then we're being followed on foot."

"Which makes it even creepier," said Lily. "Can you narrow it down?"

I could. My neck tingled when I saw a man near a coffee kiosk, stirring a paper cup over and over. People rushed past him, but he seemed planted. I realized that from where he stood, he could see the whole big room. He wore a rumpled green jacket, baggy jeans, sneakers. The outfit was so normal, it seemed a kind of camouflage. But it was his doughy, dull face that gave him away. You don't nearly get killed by someone and not carry his face with you forever.

"It's Doyle."

Lily followed my gaze and shuddered. "Oh, my gosh. It's him! Darrell, Wade, don't look now, but look over there, but don't make it seem like you're looking over there, so don't actually look, but look who it is."

Wade stepped forward and picked up a thick guide-book from the nearest rack. He pretended to read it but glanced over and groaned. "He looks so . . . regular."

Every few seconds Doyle would stop stirring his drink to check his watch.

"Julian said our phones are good," said Lily. "If he's right, and he usually is, how does Doyle know we're here?"

"Does it matter right now?" Wade said. "He knows."

"Should we run?" said Darrell. "Or attack him? Or call the police? Or just attack him? I kind of vote to attack him."

"Which goes against absolutely *everything* Roald and Sara told us," said Lily. "Still . . ."

"We have to throw him off somehow," I said. "We may have lost the black-car goons, but this creep is slippery, like Terence said. He pops up like a gopher."

"That's why they hired him." Darrell glanced at the ticket line. "Mom's next at booth three. We'll find out soon where we're going."

Wade paid for the guidebook. "Uh-oh, he's coming this way."

"I have a plan," said Lily. "Well, I think I have a plan." She looked around and settled on a handful of teenagers on the other side of the newsstand. Then she plucked two London souvenir caps from a nearby rack and turned to the clerk. "These two, please." She paid for them, then slapped one on my head and the other on Wade's. She laughed like a crazy girl as she switched the caps back and forth. "Good, he sees us."

"Yeah, real good, Lily," said Darrell. "Now we have to attack him—"

"Keep those caps on and come with me." She pushed us all over to a group of boys and girls at the back of the newsstand, just out of Doyle's line of sight. She said something to them. They nodded with a laugh. Then she slid our hats off our heads and sat them on one of the boys and a girl with a ponytail. Clever. They didn't look like us, but were about the same height. The kids turned and walked away, switching caps, then switching them back, laughing loudly.

"What is all this—" Darrell started.

"Shh." Lily kept us behind the newsstand, then peeked out. "It worked. I told them to laugh to attract attention. It worked. Look!"

You could almost see Doyle jump with joy when he

spotted our decoys pass under an arch and enter the platform area. Looking both ways, he dumped his coffee cup in a receptacle and skulked quickly after the kids. When they entered an open train car, he paused a few seconds, bowed his head, then did the same.

"Yes!" I said. "Lily, you are awesome!"

"Simple, but effective," she said. We moved up outside the platform arch. "I hope Doyle doesn't mess with those nice kids. Maybe they could take him."

The doors whisked closed on the train. Then, just as it began its roll out of the station, the girl with the decoy cap turned in her seat. I watched Doyle. He saw her and spun around in a rage, and started moving back through the carriage.

"He knows and he's mad!" I said. The train soon picked up speed and was out of the station, too far for me to see any more.

Wade checked his watch. "He'll get out at the next stop and come back, but we'll be gone. He'll have to track us all over again. Nice work, Lily."

Darrell breathed out. "I second that. And I think the kids will be all right. The muscly one playing me looked like he could take Doyle. Here's Mom—"

Sara had a strange look on her face when she hurried over. "I was like a spy, saying the words Terence told me to say. The woman at the counter blinked, then said, 'The London Midland line doesn't go to Bishops Stortford. You want to go here.' And she pulled out an envelope with tickets from under the counter."

"So cool!" said Darrell. "Terence has people everywhere."

"He must," Sara said. "The cashier said that because of Becca's German puzzle, Terrence suggests we to go to a place called Bletchley Park and ask for someone named Renji. Our train leaves in nine minutes."

When we told her about Archie Doyle, Sara went red with anger—for Doyle and for us—then pulled us into a tight group. I expected her to rip up the tickets and say we were going to forget about the relics. She didn't.

"We have to take care of ourselves. Of one another. If we do, they can't stop us. We *can't* be stopped. . . . I love you all so much, you know. Now come on."

That was it. She was done.

With only a few minutes before our train was to leave, we headed onto it and took our seats. They were comfortable, clean, bright green, and new. We settled right in, breathless and rattled, but safe. Wade was the first to speak.

"Renji is a mysterious name," he said. "Sounds African or Japanese, maybe?"

Lily waved her tablet. "Renji Abarai is the name of a Japanese manga character. But he's fictional, so it's probably not him."

"Probably," said Darrell. "But Becca might see him in a trance."

"Her trances are not fictional!" Lily protested. "They're not, right?"

"Right," I said with a laugh. After the Doyle thing at the station, it was strange how quickly we got to talking and joking as if we were regular kids. It amazed me that we could bounce back so quickly, but I found myself wanting to put *the horror* away. And the warning. And the blackouts.

"Bletchley Park"—Sara said, scanning the guide-book Wade bought at the station—"was the top secret setting for British code-breaking activities during the Second World War. That's why Terence is sending us there. The men and women who worked there broke German codes and ended the war years sooner than it would have ended otherwise. That's not at all fictional."

A series of beeps sounded, then the doors on our car closed with a breath. The train began to roll smoothly out of the station, as if it rode on rubber wheels.

I breathed in and out slowly, and my pulse eased its rapid drumming. Archie Doyle and the Order weren't an immediate threat. My nose was dry. I felt better.

After all the running, we were in a comfortable train on our way to a place called Bletchley Park in the English countryside to meet a mystery person by the unlikely name of Renji.

CHAPTER THIRTEEN

I don't want to say that because the Order was after us, we were scared of the world. But we did have to be alert to what was around us. We had to observe and be careful. We had to notice everything or risk becoming victims.

Darrell would say we were leading the spy way of life. He'd be right.

Like on that train to Bletchley.

Without anyone suggesting it, the four of us—and Sara, too, now—had settled into two benches across the aisle from each other and facing opposite ways to allow us to see both ends of the car at the same time.

Lily and I sat with a view back toward London; the others sat across the aisle and looked forward. In case we needed to escape, we sat close to a set of doors.

Getting out of London was a good thing; my pulse slowed right down. Until I felt a trickle in one nostril and turned my face to the window. I took a napkin from my pocket and raised it to my nose. Only a drop. I put the napkin away.

"Um . . . guys? In my latest vision . . ."

"Did you see him again?" asked Darrell, leaning over Wade.

"Tell us," said Lily.

"It was the day Thomas More was executed. We were in the Tower of London. His cell. Nicolaus told me the names of the horrors he discovered on his second journey. I looked them up. They're really awful. A rebellion in China in 184 AD. A war in Europe in the seventeenth century. A huge famine in Ukraine in 1933, really huge. Millions died. Nicolaus said he didn't go any farther into the future after he saw what he had done . . . what his time traveling had caused."

Lily looked me in the eyes. "Wait. You don't think you're doing the same thing, do you? By going back in your mind?"

"I don't know."

"I do. You're just passing through back there. Browsing, not buying."

Wade was suddenly out of his seat, walking down

the whole length of the aisle, then back again, without going anywhere. He wasn't looking at passengers, not even at his watch. His face was all frowny. I leaned back with Lily.

"Plus, I'm kind of embarrassed by these vision things," I whispered.

She laughed quietly. "You're *embarrassed*? I don't know what that means. I've never been embarrassed. Besides, we'd be useless without the clues you get when you go zombie. Just kidding. But what are you even talking about?"

"Not that it happens. But talking about it. I don't think he believes me." Wade had paused at the other end of the car. His lips were moving.

"You're joking, right?" she said.

I breathed in slowly. My nostrils were dry. "I can't make it sound real. It's like hocus-pocus. All fantastic and magical. It's like, 'Look at me. I'm having visions from the past, so you have to take me seriously.' But he's all numbers and can't believe any of it. As if it's believable, anyway."

Lily glared at me as if I were Darrell making a dumb joke. "Are you done? Because first of all, we *don't* think any of that. Becca, you are *so* not flaky or . . . how do I put this . . . funny. We *all* take you seriously because

104

it's what we have to do. Second, who cares what Wade thinks? Third, he doesn't even think that."

"I see him staring at me—"

"Because he *likes* you, dummy!" she hissed in my ear. "And he's *worried* about you and *believes* what you're telling him, and *if* he's having a hard time with your cryptical magical time-travel visiony thing, it's because he's trying to make his brain understand how you fit in with all his numbers, which he's been nuts about since before he was born, and here you are shaking up his world but because he's a boy all he can do is stare at you, if that makes any sense, which I think it does, but I'm not really sure."

I felt like laughing or hugging her, but Wade suddenly stormed through the aisle and plopped down in the seat next to me. "I have a problem," he said.

Glancing at Lily, I said, "A problem? I knew it—"

"It's like this," he said, not looking at me but at the ceiling of the car. "You saw Copernicus in 1517—and it had to be, right, because of all the Thomas More evidence—but you said Copernicus told you about *both* 1527 *and* 1535. So he must have seen those things on his journey."

"The second journey," I said. "When he saw the problems he thinks he made."

"Right. His second journey. But . . ." He trailed off. He clamped his eyes shut, pursed his lips like he was going to play trumpet. Or explode. Either one.

Then he opened his eyes. "Copernicus took a third journey."

"What? No. He told me only two."

"He obviously must have taken a third journey," Wade said. "He told you that he didn't go forward in time after he saw Holodomor in 1933. But he also knew who you were. It's so simple. He couldn't have known about you unless he came up to the present on a third journey. Which makes me think he wasn't talking about some 'nightfall' in the past but about tonight."

I stared at him. "I . . . so he went a third time. Maybe he made a mistake."

"Mistake? Copernicus? No way," Wade said, fixing me with his eyes. "He contradicted himself, plain and simple. And why would he do that? Don't even answer, because I already know why. Because he's giving us another clue!"

I kept staring back at him. "What kind of clue is that?"

He tore his eyes from me and turned to Lily. "You see. Lily, you see it, right?"

Surprisingly, she nodded. "I kind of do. But we won't

really know until tonight at the Tower of London. But then *why* did he go? If he realized from his second journey that horrible things had happened after his first, and would probably happen after his second, why in the world did he go a third time?"

"Well, that's the question, isn't it?" Wade said. "It's another clue for us."

My head started to pound, but it wasn't a blackout coming on. It was because Wade had realized something, and it was big. It was huge. And it was dark.

"Nicolaus didn't lie to fool me," I said. "He wants us to keep searching, so finding Crux must be a good thing. But maybe two people will die anyway."

The train stopped at Watford Junction, and now Darrell came over. "I heard some of what you said. To me, the big thing is to keep searching. The bad thing happens anyway. But if we find Crux, we can do some good. If that's true, then the most important thing now is to solve the puzzle Copernicus showed you."

Sara had been resting during all of this, but she was looking over now and nodding. "That does sound right. Becca, what can you remember about it?"

"Well, it was pretty complex, with lots of symbols. Some were old German letters. Most of them I've never seen before."

Darrell sat himself opposite and stared into my eyes. Lowering his voice, he said, "Rebecca Moore, think of nothing else. Listen to my words. And remember. The fate of the world hinges on what you remember right now—"

"Darrell, don't scare her," Sara said. "Let the poor girl breathe."

I glanced at Wade, who was quiet during all of this, just biting his lip.

Then I closed my eyes and tried to bring up the puzzle in my mind. Don't ask me how my brain did it, but it did. Out of the haze in my head was the image Nicolaus had shown me, in all its detail, a pizza of strange symbols. There were numbers around its edge, like a clock's dial, but they were all out of order: 76, then 30, then 12 . . .

The Holbein puzzle.

It would show what happened to Crux after the death of Thomas More.

Moving back and forth between the image in my mind's eye and my notebook, I drew everything he showed me. By the time I finished, the train had made three more stops—Hemel Hempstead, Berkhamsted, and Leighton Buzzard—and was on its final leg to Bletchley. There was nothing more to draw.

Sara leaned over the image and blinked. "You're

pretty sure that this is what Nicolaus showed you in Thomas's room in the Tower?"

"I am," I said.

Unfortunately, no one had the slightest idea of what we were looking at.

CHAPTER FOURTEEN

"It's as exact as I can make it," I said. "I'm amazed I could remember it. But really, it's very close."

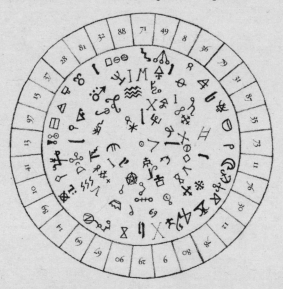

"Right," said Wade. "But close to *what*?" He didn't say it snottily.

"I don't know." I shut my eyes to see if there was anything I'd forgotten. I envisioned Nicolaus in the prison cell's candlelight. No. There wasn't anything else. "This is it. Pretty exactly. A handful of Gothic letters, some Latin ones."

Sara studied it. "Aren't some of them astronomical symbols, too?"

Wade nodded his head slowly. "This thing that looks like a tilted number four"—he pointed at one—"is *kind of* like the symbol for Jupiter. But there's also an hourglass and a kite, a diamond, some *X*s. Maybe from alchemy."

"The Latin letters could all be Roman numerals," said Lily.

Sara smiled. "Good. Alchemy. Astronomy. Gothic letters. Latin. I've never seen this combination in a single document."

"So it's a kind of mash-up of different things," said Darrell. "We've done mash-up before. Someone will solve it. Not me, of course. Maybe Renji can."

The train began to slow, and a female computer voice came over the address system: "The next station stop is Bletchley."

I closed my notebook, stood up, and stretched. "I hope so."

As we gathered our things, we were instinctively on alert again. A safe, comfortable, murder-free ride had come to an end, and we were targets once more. Pushing out onto the open platform, I studied everyone: three women in business suits standing by themselves, a few middle-aged couples, one father wrangling two young children while an infant slept in a pack on his chest, and one older couple, the woman leaning on a walker.

"All clear," Sara whispered, waving her guidebook. "Bletchley Park closes at five, and it's nearly four, so we need to move along."

We climbed the stairs to the bridge over the tracks and exited the station on the other side into a small parking lot. Right away, we spotted the sign—Bletchley Park—with an arrow pointing up the road to the right.

The sun was far past its peak but falling slowly, and even though it had been chilly in London, the air here was warm and smelled of green lawns and summer. The trees were in leaf, and little yellow flowers waved along the borders of the road. It was so astonishing to find myself so quickly out of the dangerous twisted city and into the warm countryside of an English novel, that it seemed impossible anything bad could happen here.

Which I knew made it completely possible.

"The Germans used a coding machine called the Enigma," said Sara. "It produced billions of variations and was very difficult to decrypt, but the people gathered here—cryptographers and mathematicians—were able to crack it. Terence could be having us meet an expert in German codes and puzzles."

"Good," said Lily, searching on her tablet now. "The machine they built to figure out Enigma was called the Bombe, a mechanical calculating machine—"

"Alan Turing invented the Bombe," said Wade. "I remember Dad telling me about him. He's like the father of computers. Lily, if it wasn't for Alan Turing, your hands would be holding nothing right now."

"Oh, they'd be holding something," she said. "I just wouldn't show you."

"Ha!" said Darrell. "I don't know what that means, but I like it."

A ray of sun shot through the trees directly into my face. I was startled for an instant, but it wasn't a blackout coming on, it was the sun. And since we'd covered our tracks pretty well with Archie Doyle, my only goal was to find out everything I could about Holbein's puzzle.

***

The gate to Bletchley Park was bordered by a guard-house, where a man pointed us to a low, rambling cinder-block building called Block B. The ticket booth was inside, along with a bookstore and gift shop. While Sara purchased entry tickets, Darrell mustered up courage to ask the clerk, "Is anyone named Renji here?"

I had my doubts, but the nice woman behind the ticket counter twitched excitedly. "How on earth did you know that? It's rather a secret when they come, you know, and so delicious when one shows up. She's just popped into the library at the main house. You can't miss her."

"So Renji is a woman?" asked Sara.

"Of course!" she said. "All the Wrens were. Among the many people here during the war with Turing and Dilly Knox and the rest were thousands of young women." She leaned over—"They did much of the real work, you know"—then leaned back. "The *G* stands for Gorley. Mavis Gorley. But everyone back then called her Wren G, so we do too. Lovely dear lady is our Wren Gorley!"

"One mystery solved," said Lily. "A hundred thousand to go."

"Thanks so much," Wade said. "We can't wait to meet her."

We took a paved path around a small, sun-dappled lake and headed toward the big main house, a rambling, arch-windowed brick mansion trimmed in white stone. It had a green copper dome on one end and an arcade and octagonal tower on the other, with a cluster of chimneys and gables in between.

It was charming, and odd, and homey, all at the same time.

"I already love this place and want to live here," I said.

"Something told me you would," Sara said as her phone rang. She answered it and listened. "Yes, Terence. Good. Tell him to be careful." She hung up. "Your father and Terence will be here soon. Roald is driving. On the wrong side of the road for him, and, well, crossed fingers that he and Terence make it in one piece."

We passed between two winged statues and under a shaded arch into the mansion. It smelled of wood and paper and everything old. On our left was a large, hushed room lined with glass-fronted bookcases, obviously the library.

Five desks were set up in a kind of semicircle facing us, a bay of large windows behind them, from where the sun shone down into the room, warming the carpet. The desks were fitted out with old telephones, typewriters, stacks of papers, hooded lamps, maps, and coffee cups, as if their occupants had just been called away to hear a breaking radio broadcast or an emergency briefing. The Second World War could still be on in this room. You could feel the history of thousands of people busily working in the blocks and huts—many of them young women—where breaking the enemy code was serious business. It struck me that we were doing the same thing: cracking codes, saving the world.

I felt strangely at home in that room.

And so did someone else.

Bent nearly in half over one of the desks was a tiny white-haired woman, mumbling to herself and tapping a pencil on the rim of a flowered teacup.

"Hello?" Sara said.

"Hush!" The woman had a newspaper spread out on the desk in front of her. "Think, Mavis, think!" she grumbled under her breath, and reached for the cup but didn't lift it. "A twenty-letter word meaning a record of brain activity . . ."

Darrell laughed. "A twenty-letter word *is* my brain activity!"

"Ha!" the woman said, raising her eyes. "Good one, but no. Emma! Your friends are here! *And* I need a twenty-letter word for a record of brain activity!"

Your friends are here?

I heard a laugh from the hall, and a slender, short-haired teenage girl swept into the room. "Oh, I don't know, Grandmum. Probably *electro*-something—"

"Ha!" The woman bent over the puzzle again. "Electroencephalogram!"

"You're good," Wade said, and I remembered that before Galina had Wade's uncle Henry murdered, the man had used coded crosswords to alert Guardians around the world.

Emma thrust out her hand. "I'm Emma Gorley. Julian's friend. He called to say you needed help with a German code. This sparkly lady is my grandmother."

The woman set down her pen and smiled. "I worked on the Bombe, you know. The *Turing* Bombe. I'm Mavis Gorley. Welcome to Bletchley."

"We're so pleased to meet you," said Sara. "Thank you for your service."

But that was all the small talk. The moment I told her that we had something called "the Holbein puzzle," Mavis sat up sharply in her chair and her eyes narrowed.

"Hans Holbein? A brilliant cryptographer if ever there was one. As we used to say, every minute we delay is another soldier killed. Show me what you have!"

Everyone looked at me. I didn't hesitate. There was

no way—*no way*—that this delightful woman could be a friend of Terence's, and her granddaughter a friend of Julian's, and have *anything* to do with the Teutonic Order.

I knew she was on our side. How could a Wren be anything else?

"Hans Holbein made a puzzle. I saw it in a . . . dream, then drew it," I said, opening my notebook. "This isn't the original, but it's pretty exact."

I showed her what I had drawn on the train.

Mavis drew in a breath. "Oh," she said. "Oh, my dear!"

CHAPTER FIFTEEN

Mavis's face went dark, concentrated, but her old eyes glowed.

"And I thought you were going to give me something simple. This is quite fascinating. The Gothic-style letters"—she pointed them out with the retracted tip of her ballpoint—"proclaim it as indeed German, early sixteenth century. Holbein is very likely its author. The alchemical symbols are common enough."

"We think it tells the location of something Sir Thomas More called an algorism stone, which we think is code for a special box," Wade said, glancing at me. "When he was executed, we think he gave this box to his family."

"We can tell you more, but there's a bit of danger involved," said Sara.

"More than a bit," Darrell added. "There's a group called the Teutonic Order trying to stop us from decrypting this."

"By any means necessary," said Lily.

"They've already tried to kill us," Wade said.

"Kill you?" said Mavis. "Well, of course they have! You only know you're onto something if someone wants you dead. I'm trained for that, you know."

She took a huge sloshing gulp of tea, pushed her cup to the side, bent over my notebook, then jumped to her feet. "I need the photocopy machine!" She bounded across the hall, where a copier was hidden behind a narrow set of closet doors.

"Is there a restroom?" asked Sara.

"I'll show you," said Emma.

No sooner had they left the room than an elderly gentleman doddered into the library. I wondered if he had worked at Bletchley Park, too, and asked him.

"Ah, no," he said. "Thothe codebweakers were the weal hewoes."

His pant legs were clipped tightly around his calves, indicating that he had just been on a bicycle. He had a mop of bushy gray hair and thick glasses that kept sliding down his nose as he peered at the books. He grinned toothily. "Bookth! Thome of them you can't find any-where elthe in England!"

I smiled back. "It's a wonderful place, isn't it?"

"Oh, it ith," he said. "It thcrtainly ith. Ta-ta!"

After nearly knocking him down on her way back in, Mavis stormed over to us, waving a sheet of white card stock. "Scissors!" she shouted, even as she rummaged through the old drawers, wrenching them out until she had found a pair. In seconds she had trimmed her copy into a perfect circle.

"You said this was Holbein's puzzle?" Mavis asked.

"Yes—"

"Incorrect!" she said.

"But, I'm pretty sure—"

"This," she said, "is *one half* of Holbein's puzzle! It is, as you probably guessed, the base of a two-part cipher wheel. The other wheel will be smaller and fit over this one. You'll also need a key to know the sequence of turns for the top wheel. The key could be a word or a number and could, in fact, be among the symbols on this wheel. But you won't find the answer without the top wheel."

"Something else to look for," said Lily. "Is there anything you *can* tell us?"

Mavis nodded her head. "There is *some* code-breaking we can do. For instance, nine Gothic letters are interspersed with the symbols. They need to be unscrambled. There are several Latin letters here, too. They could spell a clue, or a number. For that, we will need the Bombe. And *that* is in Hut Eleven—"

"Unweth you die wight here!" said a raspy voice.

We wheeled around to see the mop-haired man with the bicycle clips on his pants. He tore off his hair and tugged out his set of false teeth.

"Archibald Doyle!" Lily gasped.

"Only me mum calls me Archibald!" he snarled. "You best call me 'the last person I saw before I died'!"

With one quick move Archie thrust Mavis aside. She collapsed gently on the carpet with a gasp. Then he lunged past all of us and stole the code wheel right off the desk!

Chapter Sixteen

Without thinking, I grabbed Doyle's outstretched hand and yanked it hard. He screamed and swung his free arm at me. Wade was suddenly there with raised forearms—a weird move, but it blocked the punch. I snatched the code wheel out of Doyle's fingers and jumped back.

Breathing hard, his face a wrinkle of pain, he drew a pistol from his tweed jacket. "Give me that thingy," he growled, waving his gun around.

I backed up. We all did. Darrell and Lily helped Mavis to her feet. Her cane was on the floor. She locked her eyes on Doyle.

"One thing I dislike very much is a *traitor*!" she snarled. "And *you*, once a proper Englishman, I presume—whose parents my code mates and I defended with our hearts during the war—have sold your soul to a foreign power!"

Doyle wiggled his gun at her, his eyes fixed on the code wheel in my hand.

"During the war, eh? We're still at war, ma'am. You"—he said to me—"give me that thing, whatever it is, or the old lady gets it."

While Lily and Darrell moved back to the window with Mavis, Wade was edging along the wall on their right. Another spy move. Spread out, distract the enemy. By now I was in the middle of everyone.

"How did you even find us?" I asked, realizing that my nose had started to bleed again. I gently slid a napkin from my pocket.

"You're the genius here; you figure it out. But don't take too long. You'll soon be dead, you will."

At that moment, Sara and Emma returned from the restroom. Emma yelled what might have been a British curse word and pummeled Doyle with her fists.

I crouched, snatched up Mavis's cane, and swatted his legs. He fell to his knees. At the same time, Mavis heaved an antique telephone at him.

Trying desperately to block it, Doyle threw up a hand—his gun hand. The phone made an ugly sound when it met his forehead, but worse was the blast from his gun. It blew a neat hole in the ceiling.

"Bletchley Park is a registered national charity, you fiend!" Mavis squealed.

Lily and Darrell now leaped at him from different sides, keeping him on the floor, while Wade tipped over one of the desk chairs and pinned Doyle underneath. Then Emma took Mavis by the arm, and we all hurried out.

Slamming the library door behind us, we stumbled into the bright outdoors. At least a dozen security officers were running across the lawn toward the mansion.

"Left!" Emma called, rushing around the house and down past a small post office and—surprisingly—a toy shop, right into a pack of visitors and a guide.

"Scatter!" I yelled. "There's a killer chasing us!"

You'd be surprised, but that did nothing at all. People gave us looks as if we should mind our own business. Even the presence of a near-ninety-year-old woman running—*running!*—didn't seem to alarm them.

Then they saw Archie, who must have overturned the chair and squeaked by the guards, busting out a side window. He huffed past the post office with a gun in his hand, and someone decided to scream.

"Aw, you hush!" Archie snapped, firing into the air.

Darrell ran with his mother. Wade rushed ahead with Mavis and Emma. Lily and I followed. We could hear yelling now, followed by another gunshot.

"This way!" Emma called, reminding me of Meg and Bucklersbury. We pushed into a closed-in yard that housed a rambling stretch of redbrick buildings. A long, low bungalow stood on one side, a string of cottages on the other.

"Gran, where to?" Emma asked.

"The garages," said Mavis, pointing to a bank of open bays behind us. "We Wrens used to get the soldiers to give us lifts into town in their trucks. It wasn't hard to convince them, after all. Everyone, inside—"

We piled in. It was dark in there, but I could make out three or four restored antique cars, their moonlike hubcaps gleaming. Moments later, I heard footsteps rustling the gravel outside the garages, and we immediately crouched behind an old troop truck. Doyle crept past the nearest open bay, silhouetted against the light. He swung his pistol like a gunslinger, slowly side to side.

"You can't run away from me!" he growled from the opening.

"How did he get away from security?" I whispered.

"They don't carry guns," Emma whispered back. "Boys, come with me." She nodded to the back of the garage, where a narrow door stood halfway open. While the rest of us stayed put, Emma, Wade, and Darrell inched out the back door.

Doyle remained in the garage-bay opening. Then Lily slipped away and went out the back, too. *Thanks a lot.* It was only Sara, Mavis, and me now.

My heart pounded faster. My head throbbed, felt suddenly heavy, then light as a balloon. *Please, not that, not now.* Archie stepped into the garage. All at once, I saw Emma and Wade tiptoe across the yard behind him. Emma purposely scraped her shoes on the gravel. Archie spun around, but Wade was ready with a handful of gravel to his face. Archie fired wildly. Then Lily and Darrell were there with the security guards. While the guards wrestled Archie down, we dashed across the yard and were hurrying past a memorial to Polish code breakers when Sara's phone rang.

"Roald? Where are you—" More shots thudded from the yard. "Mavis, my husband's here—"

"Tell him to head to the Block B parking lot!" Mavis hooted. She took hold of Sara now. "This way!" She toddled off among the greenery. "In case the traitor gets free again, we'll lose him among the huts. Here. Hut Eleven!"

Sara whispered into the phone, while Mavis pushed into a low wooden structure, like a single-story barn, where the code people had worked during the war. Sara, Lily, and I followed, while Emma, Wade, and Darrell stopped short.

"We'll stand guard," Wade said.

"Only we won't be standing," said Darrell. "We'll be spying." They darted around the back of the hut.

"Emma's nice," I said to Lily when we got safely inside. "I'm not sure I like her just splitting off with the guys, though."

"You're not sure?" Lily said. "I'm sure. I *don't* like it. We're the team. The four of us. Oh, no. I'm positive I don't like it."

"Girls," said Sara. "Some help, please?"

The tables inside Hut 11 were piled with books and papers and folders, old phones, even an original Enigma. Mavis told us that the hut had been dressed for a television show about the Wrens and had just been in a film. Behind the desks stood a massive rectangular machine about seven feet tall. It was, Mavis said, "the Bombe." The front was fitted with over a hundred color-coded circular drums in columns and rows. "Rotors," Mavis called them. The open back side was a complete snarl of wires and pins and circuits.

Mavis stood in front of it and seemed lost in history. "The thrill of building and using this magnificent device . . . Alan, Dilly, all the rest of us . . . "

Then she was back with a start. "Now, then. Without the top wheel of the Holbein puzzle, the characters on the bottom wheel are no more than an alphabet soup of symbols and letters. We'll need the Bombe to help us narrow down the possibilities of letter combinations. So . . ."

For ten solid minutes, Mavis grumbled and groaned, beamed and frowned over the German letters, scratching the characters on a pad of paper, erasing, then rescratching. Then, after studying the drums on the front side, she busied herself rewiring the back until her old fingers couldn't manage, so she enrolled Lily and me to connect the wires where she told us to.

At last, Mavis said we were ready.

"Ready?" said Sara. "For . . ."

"For this!" Mavis flipped several switches on the left side of the cabinet, and the rotors began to turn. The roar of the machine at full tilt was incredible. Like a jet engine warming up. The drums spun around at different speeds, the top row going fastest, the second row down moving once every rotation of the top row, and so on. It was almost hypnotic.

Lily and Sara looked at me anxiously.

"This is what we did, you see," Mavis said softly. "Hundreds like me, from 1939 to the end. It was a grand time. A serious time, of course. But so exciting."

When, after a couple of minutes, the Bombe's rotors stopped, Mavis took a deep breath. She copied out a sequence of letters, then sat at a second machine that looked very much like an old typewriter. Only this one had lights, wires, and wheels on it in addition to the keyboard and another set of letters.

This was the Enigma.

One by one she tapped in the letters she had gotten from the Bombe. A second keyboard lit up with a different letter than the one she pressed on the keyboard. She wrote those on her yellow pad. Finally, she was done.

"Hmm," she said. "I believe it is an old Hanseatic code. The German letters *A-B-E-E-H-I-L-L-L* are scrambled, but there are two possibilities the Bombe has found. *Halle*, which means, well, 'hall,' and *blei*, which means 'lead.' A hall of lead, perhaps. Sounds most eerie. From the Latin letters, we have *VID* and *VIVIM*, which translates to 'Vid lives,' if that makes sense. I'm less sure about these. There are also three *X*s. Possibly a number, a location, coordinates—"

There was a tap on one of the windows, and we saw Emma and the boys creeping low past it, gesturing frantically to the door, as if to say, *He found you!*

I couldn't stand the idea of it, but there was no option. "We have to block the doorway," I whispered. "Lily!" We grabbed both ends of a table and lifted it.

"The BBC is going to be quite miffed," said Mavis. "But this is war!"

Just before we turned the table on its side, Mavis

snatched the heavy Enigma off it. "This really *is* priceless!" she said. We overturned the table, and the telephone and papers and everything slid to the floor with a crash, but it barricaded the door. We shot toward the back, while Archie hurled himself through the front of the hut. He came in too quickly to stop. He struck the table and went head over heels over it. Mavis lowered the Enigma on his head, and he collapsed in a heap to the floor.

The back door of the hut swung in suddenly, and Darrell appeared. "All aboard the escape train!"

By the time we staggered out of the hut, alarms were going off across the Park. Then we heard a loud snapping and popping coming toward the entrance. It was a small car that looked as if it had been in the same war as Mavis had. Both side mirrors were broken and dangling from wires. There was a serious dent in the passenger-side fender. The exhaust was smoking, the engine clattering.

"Dad!" said Wade. "And Terence!"

Mavis breathed hard, then finally hung on Emma's arm. "Even I have my limits. Go, Sara, children. Search hard for the rest of the Holbein puzzle!"

Roald jumped from the car and wrapped his arms around Sara. "My gosh—"

"We have to get back to London, ASAP," I said.

"Get in. I'll drive," Roald said.

"Please, Dad, look at the car," said Wade. "We're too young to die."

Then, against all odds, Archie was there, his face bruised, his hair a mess, yelling and firing wildly. Terence jumped into the driver's seat. He jammed his foot on the gas and tore straight at Archie, spinning around in a screeching doughnut at the last second. The car struck an iron fence post. The exhaust exploded with a cloud, and the rear bumper sailed off, right into Archie.

He flew—slightly—through the air and landed in a heap.

Wade howled. "Serves you right!"

Emma hooted, and Mavis cheered from the edge of the parking lot, where a team of security guards appeared, their batons drawn on Archie. Terence gunned the engine and swung the poor car around. We dived in. He punched the gas, and we raced away. As the guards charged Archie like an attacking army, he ran after us, still shouting. "You'll never escape me in the long run!"

Maybe not, I thought as we tore out of Bletchley Park, *but we did this time.*

CHAPTER SEVENTEEN

We motored at top speed back to London in the shot-up, bumperless, too-small car, and finally approached the city a little over an hour later. We were running out of time. The day was ebbing fast, it was sprinkling, lights were coming on.

Wade had worked on the Latin the whole way with his father, not getting very far. "If we put aside the *VID VIVIM* possibility—if it's not words at all, but numbers—it still doesn't work out."

"The numerals IIVIVMVXDXX aren't a single number," his father said.

"Plus, nightfall's going to be here before we know it," Darrell said. "If something is going to happen, it'll happen soon. Come on, people. Two dead. What does it mean?"

"Ackkk!" said Lily. "We need . . . we need . . . Simon! We need Simon Tingle. Mr. Memory. If he can't help us put these clues together, no one can. Do you think we can call him? We need his brain. Terence, are our phones okay?"

"They really are," Terence said. "I'm certain your phones are not how Archie Doyle found you. Go ahead, make your call."

"He gave me his number this morning," I said. I went through my pockets, fished out his scrap of paper, and made the call. I expected the same buoyant voice and electric enthusiasm he showed in his office, but when he answered, I wasn't sure it was even him.

"Simon," I said, hitting the speaker button, "we could really use your help."

"What? What?" Simon barked into the phone. "Oh, it's you." He seemed angry. He was outside. I heard traffic.

"We've got a couple thousand questions," Darrell said.

"I can't talk." He sounded like he was in a tunnel now, on the move. His voice went in and out as if he were running. "Someone's after me. A car."

My blood trilled in my veins, went cold. "Simon? Not a black car?"

"They're all black!" he said.

"Simon," said Roald, "you need to hide somewhere. We'll find you. We're approaching London now. We've seen that car. Name a time and place."

Simon growled unintelligibly into the phone. When Roald asked if he was all right, he didn't answer at all. Street traffic crackled through the speaker.

Lily leaned over. "Simon, are you there? This is Lily, the blond one—"

"I know who it is! I remember voices!" Buses roared by him. A distant siren.

"Simon, where are you?" Sara asked. "We'll meet you anywhere you want."

There was a long pause. I heard the blare of car horns in the background and the *zip-zip* of motorcycles. "Twenty minutes, the column in Paternoster Square. Twenty minutes. If you aren't there, I'll be gone!" The call clicked off.

"Paternoster in twenty minutes," said Terence. "That will be tough. Hold on."

He was a good driver on the wrong side of the street, but we still barely got there in time, screeching to a stop on Ave Maria Lane. Terence stayed with the car, while we rushed into the square. It was sundown, the work-day over, and the square was crammed with people even in the rain, but it was easy to spot Simon, circling the column like a madman, checking and rechecking his watch. He was heated when we got to him, out of breath, and not happy.

"Well?" he said sharply, wiping rain from his cheeks. "What do you want?"

"Simon, where did you see the car?" Terence asked.

"Cars. There are at least three of them. No plates. They're everywhere."

"Should we call a friend?" asked Sara. "Sir Felix, maybe?"

"Sir Felix!" he gasped. "That's a devil of an idea!" His eyes were wild, and he started to step away. "You know, you'd better toddle off. They'll see you, too."

"We need you!" I said. "We need to make some serious connections, and you're the only one who can help us. You have a chance to save lives."

"To *save* lives?" he said. "I mostly take them, you know. I analyze information and come to conclusions. They kill people based on my conclusions. That's what MI5 does, you know."

"MI5?" Roald said. "But I thought you're with the university."

"And you have a lot to learn," Simon said. "They employ experts like me. To ferret out secrets. To know things. I'm quite an asset, I am. Or rather, my horrible, unstoppable brain is."

That paused conversation for a few seconds.

"This isn't like that," Sara said finally. "It's different. Please help us—"

"Then let's get moving. A moving target has more of a chance."

He power walked away from us, heading west. "For heaven's sake," he called over his shoulder, "ask me what you want! Do you expect me to guess?"

As we hurried to keep up with him, the inquisition began, us badgering him with all the questions we needed answers to, while Sara and Roald hung back and let us go for it, since we had figured out nearly everything so far.

"We have three scrambles. We don't know what they mean," Wade said.

"Of course you don't," he snickered. "What's the first one?"

I spelled out the letters. "*A-B-E-E-H-I-L-L-L*. Possibly German, hall of—"

"Of course it's German. *Bleihalle. Bleihalle* means 'hall of lead,' or 'lead hall'—possibly Leadenhall. It's a street." He glanced over his shoulder. "Fifteen minutes back that way. What are the Latin letters?" Wade told him what we thought were Roman numerals. "Hmm. Let me work on them. Next?"

"Does Leadenhall Street have anything to do with

Thomas More?" Lily asked.

"Ha, yes, now we get to it!" Simon said, barreling into a strolling couple. They both yelled at him, but we were already crossing the street. "Leadenhall is where German merchants did their business in London. As a member of the king's privy chamber, Thomas More would have had extensive dealings with German trades-men. The merchants were called the Hanseatic League. They were the heart of German trading activity in London."

"Like the Hanseatic Walk?" asked Lily. "We were there this morning."

"Yes, like the Hanseatic Walk where you were this morning. Next?"

"How about someone named Kratzer, a German astronomer?" I asked.

Simon looked both ways at the next corner, stepped off the sidewalk. "Nicolaus Kratzer was the king's astronomer. He taught More's children. By the way, the jumbled numerals resolve to a limitless number of dates, but I'll take a stab that the only one that interests you is *VI, VII, MDXXXV*, or the sixth of July 1535, the date on which Thomas More was executed on Tower Hill. Next?"

"Hans Holbein," I said. "The painter. Did he—"

"Holbein!" he snarled. "This is so easy! We've come

full circle. Hans Holbein painted portraits of many Hanseatic members, was a dear friend of Thomas More, and died in October or November 1543, likely from the plague. According to his biographers, and I quote, 'He was almost certainly buried either in the church of Saint Andrew Undershaft or in Saint Katharine Cree, both of which still stand'—*ta-da!*—'in *Leadenhall* Street.' Anything else?"

"That's it!" I said, turning to the others at the next crossing. "Thomas gave the algorism box to Margaret Clement," I whispered. "She knew to give it to Meg. In her grief, Meg gave the box to Holbein. He created the puzzle to show that he meant to keep Crux and have it buried with him. His puzzle points to his tomb in the church. Thank you, Simon, you did it!"

"Wait!" he said.

Then he came up to me and laid his hand firmly on my shoulder. His eyes burned—it was creepy—then he ran his fingers up toward my neck.

"Simon?" said Sara.

I started to pull away when he clutched the strap of my bag and yanked at it.

"What are you doing?" I said.

"Removing this." Simon lifted his fingers. They held a tiny silver dot plucked from the underside of the strap. "Military-grade tracking device. I noticed it this morning when you came to me. I didn't know what to make of it then. But that's how he always knows where you are. And now, where I am."

"Who does?" asked Roald as he stamped on the bug. "Archie Doyle?"

All at once the light changed, and traffic moved behind Simon. He shuddered. His eyes, on fire a second ago, went cold, glasslike. The front of his shirt turned red. I screamed. Simon crumpled forward into Roald's arms. A black BMW without plates raced away from the intersection. A pistol with a silencer withdrew inside the open tinted window as it sped off.

"They shot him!" Lily cried. "They shot Simon!"

Roald lowered Simon to the sidewalk. "Someone call the police. And Terence!" We knelt next to Simon while Sara made the calls.

"An ambulance is coming," Roald said. "But Simon, why? Why you?"

Simon breathed rapidly, his eyelids flickered. His lips curled. "Why? Because I'm . . . *The Man Who Knew Too Much*. Hitchcock 1934, remake, 1956 . . ."

His lips stopped moving, but they remained open, and his face twisted in pain. We were clustered there for several minutes, waiting for help, when we saw the BMW circling around the block. Suddenly, Terence was there in the beat-up rental car, weaving between the car

140

and us, nudging it out of range.

At the same time, my phone rang. It was Julian. "Dad told me what's just happened. I'll meet you anywhere, but you have to get out of there now!"

"I'll stay for the ambulance," Roald said.

We could already hear sirens nearing. The crowd gathering around us kept growing. It was too dangerous to remain there. We told Julian where to meet us as we hurried away, backtracking through the wet streets, heading for Leadenhall.

CHAPTER EIGHTEEN

"Horrible . . . horrible . . . horrible!"

Sara said it as we rushed from the scene. Or Lily. Or maybe I did. I don't remember who it was, but the word crashed into my ears and turned my blood to ice.

The horror was happening. Simon might survive, but the attack on him was ruthless and sudden and terrible and wrong. I wanted to scream, but had no voice. It seemed like everything was falling apart, exploding into a thousand pieces, even as things were starting to come together and we drew closer to solving the mystery and discovering Crux.

"The bug is how they found our safe flat," said Darrell, in barely a whisper. "And how Doyle tracked us to

Bletchley, despite our trick at the station."

"But who bugged you?" Wade asked. "I mean, who was even close to you? If Simon saw the bug on you this morning . . . where had you been?"

"Westminster Abbey," said Sara. "The crowd by the embankment. Maybe Doyle was there. Then the book-shop."

"The Temple of Mithras," said Wade. "But did you get close to anyone?"

"Then Pret A Manger," Sara went on. "The univer-sity."

"I don't know," I said. "One of those places."

"Sir Felix?" said Wade. "Or did Simon put it there himself? No. I don't know." None of us did, and the idea ended there.

After twenty minutes of evasive walking, we stood on Leadenhall on the corner where it met Gracechurch. It was well past seven now and dark. While weather in the countryside had been clear, it must have continued to rain off and on all day in London, because water had pooled in the street and puddled the sidewalks. Shad-ows loomed on the slick surface of the street. I realized we weren't far from the Hanseatic Walk. From Buck-lersbury. From everywhere important to us, and to me.

At the corner of Saint Mary Axe, Julian quietly emerged from the darkness. The nighttime city blazed

143

around us, but Leadenhall was eerie, solitary, overshadowed by skyscrapers. Among them was one that looked like a fat green pickle. Julian said it was nicknamed the Gherkin. Another was like a steampunk movie set. A third was wrapped up the side in scaffolding.

Beneath all of them, a ghost of the London past, was the church of Saint Andrew Undershaft, one of the two possible sites of the tomb of Hans Holbein.

The tomb that held the amber relic, Crux. We hoped.

After we filled him in on everything Simon had told us, Julian suggested we split up to save time. "Some of us might take Saint Andrew, the others Saint Katharine Cree. Becca, you said 'after nightfall,' right? That's now."

We decided that Wade, Sara, and I would take Saint Andrew, while the others would go down the street to the corner of Leadenhall and Creechurch.

Saint Andrew was small and old, with a square tower rising over it. It struck me how much I wanted modern London to fade away and the old city to blossom. That a small relic might survive five centuries, a catastrophic fire, ten months of aerial bombing, rebuilding, and decay was almost too much to hope for.

I needed the past to be alive in that church.

I needed to find Hans Holbein's tomb.

Because it was late, all the church doors were locked.

Wade was proposing we kick them open when we saw a boy stride alongside the church, followed by a man in work overalls. They entered a narrow patio leading into the back.

"Excuse me," Sara said, hurrying after them. "Excuse me, is there any possible way that we can see inside the church?"

"Now?" The man paused at the door, jangling a set of keys. "It's closed to the public right now. We have Bible study later. Have you signed up?"

"No, but it's so important," I said, trying to be polite and eager at the same time. "We've come a long way to see it, and we have to meet a flight in the morning." It wasn't much of a lie, after all. "We're running out of time."

The man looked us over and shrugged. "What do you think, Jeremy?"

The boy with him, maybe nine or ten, pursed his lips and wrinkled his nose. "One thinks it's rather too late, Father. Sightseers should return in the morning."

The man shrugged. "There you have it, then, from the buildings manager's own son."

It was odd, as if the father took orders from the son.

"But we . . . ," I started. Then I had an idea. "We could pay a late-night sightseers' fee. Or a donation to the church. For the upkeep?"

This time the man frowned. "Well, I don't know . . ."

"In your names, perhaps," said Sara. "A hundred pounds? A donation from Jeremy and . . ."

"Tim," the man said. "From Jeremy and Timothy Larkin. I like the ring of that. I think that'll do nicely, yes. Follow us in, then."

"But Father, one hundred pounds—"

"Nix it, Jeremy. It's for the church. Come on in." He unlocked the back door, and we were suddenly in a warm, small office. It smelled of coffee and steam.

"One usually comes to see the window," Jeremy said as his father darted into an adjoining room. "It's Pre-Raphaelite, you see. Survived the Blitz. Barely."

There were sounds coming from the next room. Tim reappeared, then went into what we discovered was a kitchen. Two men were boiling something on the stove in there. Jeremy continued into the nave of the church, and we followed.

My heart sank.

Aside from a set of high arches on either side of the nave, Saint Andrew Undershaft had been completely modernized, with light wood paneling, freshly painted white walls, a cluster of cushy chairs, and tables stacked with paperback Bibles. All my visions of a mysterious old chapel were instantly dispelled.

"Are there any crypts or vaults?" Wade asked. "From

the early days. Sixteenth century. I mean, do you know where Hans Holbein is buried?"

Jeremy's eyes widened. "One thought you wished to see the window. So it's Holbein one is after? Well, one *supposes* there are vaults under the floor, of course"—he tapped his foot on the crisp new wooden floorboards—"but one has never seen them. There is no way for one to get to them. The oldest part of the church is the tower." He nodded to the corner behind us. "One cannot go there, either. Not even Father, really, and he is buildings manager. Structure's unsafe. Everything behind that door is off-limits."

"Can we see the door to the tower, at least?" Sara asked politely.

The boy sighed, as if this was taking far too long; then he walked briskly to the back end of the room. He pushed open a wooden door with a glass panel in it. "There, if one must know." At the bottom of a short set of steps stood a narrow black door. "One goes down under the new flooring, to the original floor of the tower. Or one *would* if one *could*. It's quite unsafe and hasn't been used for years—"

"Jeremy! The Bibles!"

"Coming, Father!" he called back. It was strange to hear people shouting in a church. "Father requires one's assistance to set up for Bible study tonight. In the meantime, touch nothing. One has one's eye on you."

"Yes, of course." Sara smiled. "We'll just poke around, if that's all right."

"One supposes that it's all right, if, I repeat, one touches nothing and disturbs no one." Jeremy gave us a particular glare, then spun around on his little heels toward the kitchen, muttering under his breath. We soon heard the sound of books being thumped on tables and the rattle of spoons being counted and stacked.

"I'm glad Lily's not here," Wade whispered. "One might expect a scene."

"If there *are* crypts," I whispered, "the tower might be the only way to them."

"I think we've earned at least a peek," said Sara. "I'm sure this is some kind of crime, but I'll research that later. You go. I'll stand guard. Don't die down there."

Wade and I slipped behind the glass door and down the steps. Jiggling the knob, we were able to coax the old door open. I pushed it in, and white stone dust showered my head. When it stopped falling, I looked up. Most of the steps to the tower's upper floors had collapsed, leaving holes in the stone and some planks to show where they'd been. In the light from the street leaking into the tower from the windows high up on all four sides, we saw two or three partial floors sagging overhead and an uppermost landing that seemed to hang in midair.

"Jeremy was right," Wade said. "A hundred pounds won't go very far."

"Let's go in," I whispered. "One at a time. Me first."

Holding my hand over my mouth and nose, I pressed forward. There weren't any vaults or crypts that I could see right off, but there was a short wooden door in the wall, half open, with darkness beyond. I crossed the floor and peeked around it. A narrow set of steps led down even farther. I squirmed past the door to get to them, scraping my elbows rather than touch the door. I knew it would squeak if I did. I half slid and half shuffled down the dust-covered steps.

They led into a deep chamber whose ceiling was high enough to stand under. "I think we're back under the church floor here," I whispered up the steps.

Wade was at the top of the stairs now. Crouching, he took out his phone, tapped the flashlight app, and scanned around. I did the same. Then he pointed his light over my shoulder at several silvery-gray stones set flat into the walls. They had inscriptions on them. "There. Vaults. Crypts. Becca, I think we found them."

I picked my way to the crypts. Wade started down the stairs to me. Then we heard a sound from upstairs in the church. A plate crashed. Someone ran. Jeremy yelled something, and doors slammed one after the other.

Wade started back up. "Is it Lily and the others already?" he whispered.

Sara was there at the top of the stairs. "Someone's just come in—"

Neither of them could get down to me before a light flashed across the floor behind them. They ducked back behind a wall of fallen rafters. I flattened behind a stone bench, flicked off my light, and heard the crunch of gravel under shoes. A single set of feet approached from across the upper room. They came down the steps. They were too heavy to be Lily's.

I held my breath as an intense white light shot past me to the stones on the wall and focused on them. A tall figure followed the light and stood before the stones. I peeked over the bench. My eyes adjusted to the shadows. I shivered.

Markus Wolff was in the chamber with me.

CHAPTER NINETEEN

Wolff studied the wall lit by his flashlight. I was behind him. In my mind I heard Wade screaming: *Becca! What are you waiting for? Get out of there!*

It was true. I might have slipped to safety. Wolff hadn't seen me; the door at the top of the stairs was still open. But I couldn't move. I was terrified. Of course I was. But more than that, I wanted to see—*had to see*—what Wolff would find.

Maybe I moved, or maybe I was just thinking too loudly, because Wolff suddenly spun around, flitted past me up the stairs, and kicked the door shut.

Then he bolted it fast.

"Strange to have a bar on the inside of the door, no?" he whispered in nearly unaccented English. It was a cold voice. "Come out where I can see you."

When I stood from behind the bench, he smiled slightly.

"Rebecca Moore. On the trail of another relic, are you?"

That surprised me. *Another* relic? Didn't he know that the relic was Crux? And what else would I be doing if not looking for it? More important, if *he* wasn't after Crux, why was he in the crypt? Why had he been at the river that morning?

"But of course you are." He relaxed, but kept his gun on me. "The great relic hunt." He said those words with a tone of . . . not *disgust*, but . . . *annoyance*?

"Alas, you are on the wrong track, Miss Moore. Crux was stolen by the astronomer Kratzer in 1535. He brought it to Albrecht. Galina will soon find it."

"I don't believe you," I said.

He shrugged. "Suit yourself."

There was muffled shouting from the other side of the door. Wade and Sara. The Larkin men, too. But I was trapped, and Wolff wasn't about to let me go. He turned abruptly and blew dust from one stone, revealing letters inscribed on it.

JOHN, KNOWN AS HANS HOLBEIN
1497/98–1543
PAINTER

"His vault," Wolff said. Without moving the gun, he did the same to the inscription on the vault directly alongside it. I couldn't read it, but he traced its letters under his slender fingers. He glared at it, as if he had suddenly become stone, too. Then he took out his phone and photographed the inscription. He pressed the screen once, twice, and I heard a whoosh as he sent the picture.

"To Galina?" I said. "Of course to Galina."

He stood aside for me to see the inscription.

JOAN ALEYN HOLBEIN
ORPHAN, FOUNDLING, WIFE
BORN 21 DECEMBER 1515
DROWNED 6 JULY 1535

My head buzzed. I nearly fainted. *My good daughter Joan Aleyn* . . .

That sweet little imp, Joan, died the same day as Thomas More?

So *that* was why the day was coded into Holbein's puzzle!

"But when did she become Joan Holbein?" I asked, despite myself.

He turned to me, his eyes pinpoints. "So, it is true. You have seen her. How else would you know of her existence? Galina would be quite interested."

I'd spoken before I realized. I wasn't going to tell him anything. "I read about her. Thomas More's last letter. She was Margaret's friend. Thomas adopted her."

"He did adopt her," Wolff said quietly. "Hans Holbein met her there, in More's household in Chelsea, in 1526 or so. Some eight, nine years later, she became his wife. Joan was younger than the painter by two decades, but this was common. They say she could not speak. And here. You see? The very day Thomas More was executed. Strange, yes? That this young woman should die the same day as her adopted father?"

Wolff then did a horrifying thing.

He cast a look around the chamber and found on the floor a heavy piece of iron. Slipping his pistol back in his pocket, and with his back to me, he used the iron rod to pry open Holbein's vault like a door. The shrieking was horrendous, criminal—iron and stone squealing—until there was a small explosion as the tomb coughed up five hundred years of dust. The stone now angled out about one foot. Wolff shone his light inside and reached his hand in.

I nearly vomited.

"Bones and rags," he said. "Nothing of value."

"That's Holbein's resting place," I said. "How could you do that?"

Ignoring me, he pried Joan's stone out next, producing the same excruciating clash of chisel and stone. I quickly looked around me, found a brick, and held it behind me, waiting. He swung Joan's stone out nearly completely. This time he didn't find even the traces of clothing or bone dust.

Also, no algorism box. No relic. Nothing at all. So where *was* Crux? Had Wolff been telling the truth? If it wasn't in Holbein's crypt, then where was it?

Wolff stood and sighed, his back still to me. "So," he said. "So."

There was no reason not to stop Wolff right here, I thought. I could, if I wanted to. And I wanted to. I took a silent step forward. I raised the brick over my head.

Then, as Wolff stood back, such an easy target, I saw something on the inside face of Joan's stone. An inscription, but not of words. It was a circle of complex designs carefully etched into the surface of the stone.

I knew instantly what it was. The top wheel of the Holbein puzzle! The wheel that Mavis Gorley said we needed. My brain screamed. Ten seconds before, I had thought Crux lost forever. But there was still a chance!

Wolff didn't linger over the design. He didn't even appear to see it. He searched both vaults once more, to be complete. "Alas. A dead end."

The brick was heavy in my hand. "Why do you care about the girl?"

"Is it not amusing, that of the hundreds of ships that left Prussia in 1517, one is of particular importance to you, Rebecca, another to me? One ship carried

Copernicus. The other brought the child of Albrecht to London."

I shuddered, and the brick fell to the floor with a thud. *The child of Albrecht?*

"Are you saying that *Joan Aleyn* was Albrecht's *daughter*?"

"A legend says"—he used the German words, *eine Legende besagt*—"that Albrecht von Hohenzollern had a child, orphaned when its mother died."

It was like he slapped me.

We had heard that story in London just over a week ago. In a taped recording that we'd discovered after Archie Doyle had murdered him, Boris Rubashov said that the wife of Albrecht von Hohenzollern, the Grand Master of the Order, had died, leaving behind a child. That was in February 1517.

"The astronomer Nicolaus Kratzer brought her here from Albrecht's court," Wolff said, "accompanied by Albrecht's nephew. He brought the child to More, who adopted her." Wolff slid his hand into a side pocket and brought out a small round object. He handed it to me. It was a locket.

Inside was a miniature painting of a teenage girl.

I knew it was Joan Aleyn. It was the same mute girl who had clutched Thomas's robe years before in that small room in Bucklersbury. Her expression here in the portrait was full of sorrow, grief, loss. Her eyes were dark enough to be black, looking—staring—off beyond the edge of the frame at something she could not bear to see but could not take her eyes from.

"Holbein painted it of his young wife," he said. "Alas, as you see from her dates, she died before reaching the age of twenty. Galina will be extremely disappointed."

"Why? Why is Galina interested in Joan Aleyn?"

Then the answer came to me. One answer. Maybe. If Holbein engraved a part of his puzzle inside Joan's vault, she might have taken on the algorism box from Meg. Because of the strange twists of history, Joan Aleyn— daughter of the infamous leader of the Teutonic Order himself—might have been a Guardian, even if only for a day!

How wonderful would that have been?

"So you *are* looking for the relic!" I said.

He seemed to smile, but maybe he didn't. "As to that, there is no end to searching for relics."

When he held out his hand for the miniature, I noticed that the back of the frame was hinged. Not caring that I might give him a clue, I dug open the back cover. There was nothing but a rough brown lining. I ran my finger across it.

"Look at us," he said softly. "So deep in the quiet of the past. What is it?"

"Paper," I said. "The back is lined with old paper."

As if he knew that any secret I discovered there would instantly be his, Wolff let his hand drop. "Is there anything on it? A map, perhaps? Or a message?"

Inserting my fingernail at the edge of the frame, I pried up the edge. It was stiff and nearly crumbled in my hands. The paper was crusted through with dried brown dust, dried paint, maybe, but I found an edge, and carefully lifted it.

"Words," I said. "English words. But I can only make out two of them."

"Yes?"

"It says . . . 'the evil' . . ."

With the breath he had been holding while I unfolded the crusted paper, he said, "Just so. An omen. Or a judgment upon us."

The evil.

Copernicus had said it. Even if a good thing happens, there is always . . . *the evil.* But how did he know what was written inside Joan's locket?

Raising his hand, as if our moment in the past had died, Wolff gently slid the miniature from my open palm. He reinserted the paper and pocketed it. "In the long thread of history, perhaps the young woman and Galina are related. All things have consequences, yes? A life here, a death there. The strange connections over time?"

It's all connections, I thought.

"For instance," he went on, "have your people told you that the remains of Kronos have been discovered in the cellar of an abbey in the Netherlands? Egmond, it is called. Our agents are right now removing it. Naturally, the monks had no idea what it was, but there you go. The oddities of time travel."

The oddities of time travel? I could tell you a thing or two!

When Wolff turned to gaze at the tombs, I stooped and picked up the brick. I could throw it at his gun, knock it from his fingers. Or better, smack his head as I had planned. Then his phone rang. *Yes!*

I threw the brick.

He moved like lightning. The brick crashed to the wall, knocking the phone from his hand. He swung his pistol hand out, struck my face, and cut it, and I fell backward to the floor. But his phone was in my reach. I snatched it up.

"Your evil orders!" I said, holding it in the air. "I should smash it—"

"Why don't you, Becca Moore?"

I was seriously going to crush the dumb thing when her image appeared on the screen. The face I had seen so many times. Galina Krause. In that fraction of a second, he twisted his phone away and read the text.

"I have an appointment," he said.

He suddenly looked tired, resigned. Like a soldier going into the horror of battle. Like someone who realized that today might be his last on earth. Or worse—like someone going into battle and realizing it was *not* his last. That he'd remain alive to do the same thing again and again and again.

"How do you do it?" I asked him. "How can you stand being a shadow? It hurts to be alone, doesn't it? It hurts me. Unable to connect with other people."

Wolff's features thawed for a brief moment. "I have my joys. My flat in Cheyne Walk. The keyboard works of Bach. Bartók's quartets. My Walther"—he lifted his handgun an inch—"and my son, Dieter. He will be twenty-seven this year."

I felt like I'd been slapped across the face again. "You have a son? A *child*?"

He smiled. "You are surprised."

"Well, yes!" I said. "You kill people for a living."

A slight nod of his head, almost a bow. His eyes searched the air between us. "When you live in the shadows, it is not so difficult to do the horrible thing." And the iron gaze was back. He climbed the steps and unbarred the door. Wade and Sara, who had been trying to get in, stumbled down to the floor at his feet.

"Are you going to kill us now?" Sara sneered up at him.

He seemed surprised by the question. "One tries not to kill on one's home ground. Unless ordered to." He gestured to his phone. "Your blood is on someone else's hands. For now."

Then, pocketing his Walther, Markus Wolff pushed past the astonished building manager, and his open-mouthed son, Jeremy, and was gone.

CHAPTER TWENTY

I rushed up the stairs and out of the chamber, gasping for breath. By the time I had my brain back, Darrell and Lily were in the church. Roald and Julian were huddling with Tim and Jeremy, who were this far from calling the police, while Julian busily pulled pound notes from his wallet.

"Simon's going to be all right," Darrell told us. "The shot missed all of his vital organs."

"Thank God," I said. "Listen, another part of the wheel is down there. We have to go back. We need to go into the crypt."

They all followed me down the steps. While Lily shone her light inside Joan Aleyn's tomb, I wedged myself as close as I could and copied the design into my notebook, line for line, while telling them everything Wolff had said.

"Galina's interested in the girl?" said Darrell. "What could *that* mean?"

"Galina might be related to her," I said, my hands shaking. "I can't think about it right now. This might be the last piece we need to lead us to the relic. Once we fit this wheel over the one we have, we'll know. We're almost there."

Without leaving the crypt, I ripped the drawing out of my notebook and tore the excess away to make a circle. Then I punched out three obvious holes through which the upper wheel would identify characters on the lower wheel.

"If the key is July sixth, 1535," said Darrell, "we have to use those numbers. Seven, six, one, five, three, five. The day Thomas More died."

"The day Joan died, too," I said. "That's why Holbein chose the day. He loved both of them and must have been crushed when they died on the same day. The algorism box went to Thomas's ward, then to Meg, to Joan, and finally, I hope, to Holbein—all on the same day. The complete puzzle will tell us where it is now."

"But how?" Lily said. "There are *three* holes in the top wheel but we have *six* Roman numerals on the bottom wheel, and out of the numerals on the outside there is no seven, six, one, three, or five, the numbers that make up July sixth, 1535. So how do we do it? Wade?"

I saw him trying to focus, studying the wheels. "Three holes, six numbers. We could start by combining the six numbers into three. July sixth is seven and six, or seventy-six, which *is* on the wheel. Then fifteen and finally thirty-five."

I took the bottom wheel from my bag, pinned the two wheels together, and lined up the bracket at the edge of the top wheel to seventy-six. All three holes were blank. "Uh-oh . . ."

"Wait," said Darrell. "This is England. Instead of July sixth, they call it the sixth of July. Instead of seventy-six, try sixty-seven."

I did. Three images showed through. A crown, a legless stick figure with its hands up, and a ball with ears on it. "These are alchemical symbols. Lily?"

"Searching." She quickly found a list of symbols reproduced on a website. "'A Table of Chymicall and Philosphicall Charecters,' from 1651. Close enough." She looked up the three symbols. "Well, I don't know what they mean, but they all begin with *R*—*Realgar* and *Regulus* and *Retorta*."

"Try fifteen, then thirty-five," said Wade.

I dialed the wheel to fifteen. All the symbols were

ones that began with *A*—*Acetum*, *Alembicus*, and *Aqua Fortis*.

At thirty-five, the three symbols all translated to *Hora*.

"So the first three symbols start with *R*," said Wade, "the next with *A*, and the last one with *H*. Which spells *R-A-H*. Is that a German word?"

Lily looked it up. "It means 'yard.' But maybe the answer isn't in German?".

Julian interrupted us in the chamber. "My dad followed the black car to the Tower of London. Markus Wolff's there, too, poking around the Bell Tower."

"This could be it!" said Wade. "Two dead in the shadow of the tower. Maybe there's a tower yard, a courtyard, or something to make it come together. Becca?"

The theories were coming like machine-gun fire. "The relic isn't here, so Wolff went to the Tower for the relic. Let's go!"

We gathered ourselves and raced over to the Tower in Julian's limo. As we bounded out of the car, I saw the great hulking castle, a high-walled prison, lit up with spotlights. Terence was inside its walls somewhere. So was Markus Wolff.

The Tower was closed, but a yeoman warder in a red

uniform and slouch hat was waiting for us. "The Ack-royd Foundation has arranged this. Follow me."

He took us briskly across the stones to the entrance gate, where we passed under an arch and inside the walls of the Tower. The moat—now a grassy yard outside the wall—was on our left, and it was huge.

"We'll have to look there, too. But the cell first. We have to see the cell," I said.

The warder paused at a wooden door in the corner tower, the Bell Tower, where Thomas had been held. He unlocked the door with a massive old key. Stairs coiled up in the darkness. The warder switched on a series of lights, and we climbed several flights, then went down a short passage and into a small room with a vaulted ceiling. A prison cell.

The warder turned on a lamp, and the walls shone gold. The pale white of the outside spotlights filtered through the "arrow loops," as the warder called them— narrow, cross-shaped openings in the wall—casting crosses of light on the floor.

I wondered if Thomas More had noticed those crosses and thought about Crux, the cross he'd kept secret for so long, even to the last day of his life, the cross he knew he had to pass on, the cross that became his final duty to protect, the prisoner's cross.

Together we searched the cell, touching nothing but

examining everything. This took a half hour, no more.

"Becca?" Lily stared at me with such intensity, I wanted to turn away.

"I don't know," I said.

My head began throbbing. Could anything at all still be in such a place after five hundred years? I didn't know that, either. The light from the arrow loops, as dull as it was, flashed into my eyes. I felt nauseated and checked my nose; it was dry.

"There's nothing here," Darrell said finally.

Wade nodded. "We can't even say what we're looking for. Becca . . ."

"I don't know!" I couldn't stand their looks. I turned away from them and saw a man holding a smoking oil lantern pass the cell. He looked in but didn't stop.

"I thought the Tower was closed," I said. The warder didn't respond.

"Didn't you see him?" I whispered to Lily. Without answering, she stepped away to Darrell. "Lily?" I said.

She didn't answer me.

"Hey!" No answer.

It was happening again. This time I was going back even before my friends faded from me. My neck ached, and my eyes. Everything hurt. In my mind, I stepped outside the cell and into the passage. The figure shuffled slowly away from me. "Wait," I said. "Please, sir?"

He turned, held up his lantern. I nearly fainted when I saw his face. I knew him, but then he had been nearly twenty years younger than he was now.

"Helmut Bern!" I said. "Bern? Is it you?"

Tilting his head, trying to see in the darkness, he drifted toward me, one slow step at a time. He had a beard now, gray, ragged. With an old man's eyes he squinted at my face in the lantern light. "Rebecca Moore, yes? I remember you from . . . before. Why are you here? Are you trapped, too?"

If Bern's hair was gray, his cheeks were even grayer. They were sunken like a corpse's. His eyes were ringed with black. His teeth were chipped, sharp, animal-like, and some were missing altogether. He had open sores on his lips, his cheeks, his nose. His clothes were nothing more than rags falling from his shoulders. His fingers were black, he was barefoot, and his body stank.

I glanced inside the cell, then back to him. "What happened to you?"

"I . . . I . . . couldn't find my way home. I don't know anymore where the machine is. I don't know. They released me from Charterhouse to see him die. They killed him today. I saw him on the scaffold. Thomas More. He let me stay at Charterhouse for years."

"It's July sixth?" I asked. "1535?"

"I've been trying to return home to my life," he said.

"But I need the machine that sent me here. I can't find it. It's not anywhere I go."

"Kronos? You can't find Kronos?"

His eyes rolled up until only yellow showed. "I don't know the way!"

I remembered what Wolff had said. "Egmond Abbey," I told him. "It's in the Netherlands."

"Egmond Abbey? Where is the Netherlands from here? Kronos is there?"

Bern had been part of Sara's kidnapping. He'd held us at gunpoint, shot our friend Marceline Dufort. But he was broken now, crushed. He was lost. Alone. *Loneliness*, the word that Copernicus himself had used. Maybe it was because of all the horrors that Nicolaus had told me about that I wanted to be kind to this man. To allow something good to happen. Good for Bern, at least.

"Go down to the water," I said. "Sail to the Netherlands. Kronos is at Egmond Abbey. It's the only way back to our time. Bern, can you hear me?"

He leaned toward me as if he was going to fall on me, or cry, or hug me, or all three. "Thank you," he whispered. His breath was horrific. Wetness spattered my cheeks. It surprised me that I felt his hot spit. "I won't forget this," he said. Holding up his lantern, he started to shuffle down the passage.

"Wait." I stepped after him. "Do the letters *R-A-H*

mean anything to you?"

He stopped, turned, shook his head. "They have her by the river, you know. Kratzer and the others. She's Albrecht's daughter. They'll ransom her and the relic. Kratzer knows Albrecht will pay. But they'll probably kill her first. Maybe it's not too late. Maybe it is. I'll show you, if you like."

He shuffled away, pulling the yellow light with him and me with it. I knew that "following" him was all in my mind. I was in More's cell with the others, not in the hall with Helmut Bern. There was no Helmut Bern, not anymore. By the look of him, he would die soon. He would never make it to Egmond Abbey.

It didn't matter. In my mind, he staggered out of the Bell Tower, and I went with him. It was dumb to look for Wolff or Terence or anyone from the here and now, but I did. Of course they weren't there. Only Bern and I were there.

The city of London, bustling just minutes ago, was now a silent town. Only the creaking wheels and clattering hooves, only the smell of water and the stink of death were there, burning my senses.

Helmut seemed to disintegrate with each step, but he was quicker than I thought he could be. How I tore down the streets after him and his swift yellow lamp, I can't tell, but soon I heard the tidal slosh of waves against the riverbank. Then someone screamed like an animal. I knew that voice, a howl from a young woman who could not speak. Helmut pointed vaguely. "Out there—"

"Joan!" I cried at the top of my lungs. "Joan!"

Her answering wail was cut short by a man shouting angrily in German. Kratzer? I rushed to the bank. Was I actually doing this or just in my mind? I couldn't tell what was real and what not as I stumbled to the water's edge. A hundred yards from me, a handful of men dragged a struggling girl into a boat.

"Stop!" I yelled, running on the sand, not knowing if I'd made a sound. "Stop!"

Joan fought with at least two men. One whipped out something silver from his waist. A knife. He forced her into the rowboat. She smacked his face, attacked the other man with her fingernails, tore away from both of them, was caught by a third and dragged, tripping and sliding across the sand. Her wails were terrifying. She was thrown facedown into the boat. One of the men pushed it off the sand into the water. Oars cut the surface frantically. They were rowing away.

"No!" I screamed, my feet sinking in the sand. "Joan!"

Whether she heard or not, I have no idea, but she lashed out at the man with the knife. She screamed hideously and put a hand to the front of her dress. Was she protecting something? The algorism box! Crux! The knife rose and fell, rose and fell. There was a splash, thin white arms waving frantically from the water.

"Loslassen!" the knife man cried. The other rowers swung their oars at Joan to stop her howling. They did stop it. A sickening thud, then silence.

I was in the water finally, wrenching my leaden legs forward. There was no movement on the surface where Joan had fallen in, and no sound save the ever-more-distant slapping of oars and Helmut Bern shrieking, *"Bringen Sie mich!* Take me!" He sloshed into the river, desperately swimming out to the boat.

"Joan!" I yelled, gasping for breath. "Joan!" I dived in. One arm in front of the other, kicking, flailing. The rowboat was downriver already. Bern was dragged onto it. I saw her white shape under the water, sinking away from the surface. I pushed myself down and clutched a wrist as cold as stone.

I swam and kicked my way to the bank as quickly as I could. I dragged her limp body up onto the sand. The beautiful young woman of the portrait was pale and beaten, her face purpled with bruises. A slash on her forehead bled into her eyes, over her cheeks. There was something under her dress at her waist. The algorism box Kratzer had been trying to steal. She'd kept it from him at last.

It was true. Joan Aleyn was a Guardian!

But even as I laid her gently on the sand, I realized that what I'd thought was the box under her dress was no such thing. There was a roundness at her waist.

She was . . . *expecting.*

This girl, this young woman, was going to be a mother.

Now no one else was with us. All the others—my best friends in the world—were nearly five hundred years away. I was the only one, alone with this woman.

Her face was ashy gray under the moonlight—except where her forehead and temples were slashed and bleeding, blossoming red. I pinched her nostrils closed. I'd never done this before, just seen an online video.

Holding her nose shut, I pressed my lips to hers and breathed in as hard as I could. Remembering how you alternate—pump the chest, breathe into the mouth, chest, mouth—I breathed in, then thumped my hands on her chest. Again. Again.

She jerked under me, convulsed. Water oozed from her lips, fountained out, mixing with her blood. I tipped her head to the side. Kept pumping. Then she coughed and spat river water onto the sand. She looked up at me, her face icy pale, her lips blue. I wanted to say something, but had no idea what. She groaned softly and tried to sit up.

"No, no," I said. "On your side." She spat out more water, coughing, gagging.

I cast around for something to stop the flow of blood into her eyes. My hands dug into my soaking pockets, finding nothing but the last of the wadded-up napkins I'd taken at the sandwich shop. She flinched under my touch. I can't tell you what that felt like—like touching air that touched me back. I watched, astounded, as the napkin, wet as it was, became soaked in her blood, and I felt my fingers grow moist when her blood seeped through the paper, soaking into the drops— now brown—of my blood. The ground shifted and gave under me. I swooned but held to her tightly.

"Keep this on your forehead," I said. "Press hard."

She did, her eyes now staring fully at me. In gratitude? In awe? Who even *was* I, coming to her from the future? A stray beam of moonlight flashed into my eyes. I heard the sudden roar of traffic on Lower Thames Street. Joan faded in and out. My vision, whatever it actually was, was pulling away from me. I fought it.

"Go, Joan!" I said to her, not knowing if she heard me. "Go to Holbein. He'll take care of you. Take the relic. I can't take it. Tell him to hide it in his crypt."

She was nearly invisible now. I heard Wade and Lily murmuring nearby, the echo of voices surrounded by stone. For an instant, I was overwhelmed by the smell of the damp cell I had left to follow Bern.

Then Joan clutched my wrist with her free hand, wrenching me back to her. Still holding the bloody napkin on her face, she set my hand gently on the bump at her waist. She pointed to herself and growled a word.

That growl was her name. "Joan." Then she pointed at me, her eyes wide.

"I'm Becca," I said. "Rebecca."

She nodded and touched my hand to her waist again, and it was as if someone had drowned me with icy water. It had been staring at me the whole time.

RAH

"I . . . I . . ." The sand and the river faded away. I was solidly back in Thomas More's cell in the Bell Tower. Someone was shaking me by the shoulders. I gasped and gagged. Wade slapped his palm on my back. I came to.

"Becca!" he said. "Becca, where are you?"

"What? I—"

"Terence and Julian have spotted Archie Doyle," said Sara. "He followed us to the Tower. Markus Wolff slipped away. We're supposed to wait here—"

"Sir Felix is bringing his spies to help us," said Darrell. "Two people will die here tonight. Bec, you're wet—"

176

"It's not here. It's not this tower! Tell him to meet us at Saint Andrew!" I said, my clothes soaked, my head splitting in two. "The Holbein puzzle leads back there. Crux is in Holbein's crypt! It's there!"

CHAPTER TWENTY-ONE

I told them all what I'd seen and done, while Roald and Sara urged us quickly away from the Tower and Archie Doyle, and into the winding streets back to Saint Andrew.

"Becca," Wade said, hustling next to me, "this is just—"

"Not now! I don't need to hear it's impossible. I know it's impossible. But if it didn't happen, if I didn't save her, *RAH* means nothing, and we have no relic."

I pushed ahead of Wade, ahead of everyone but Roald and Sara, up Tower Hill, that sad last climb of Thomas More, saying out loud what I should have realized ages ago. "Copernicus wasn't talking about the Tower of

London. He was talking about Saint Andrew's tower. That's where two dead will die."

"Which means Copernicus is in London right now," said Lily. "He's here."

I realized that, too.

We were breathless and frantic by the time we reached the church. A dozen armed men swarmed toward us instantly when a voice came out of the shadows.

"It's all right, officers. They're with me."

Sir Felix hustled over. The men backed off.

In a low voice, he said, "The government has set up a ring of security around the church. It's been cleared of people. My intelligence mates identified the car as belonging to a German national who consults with the government. Except on this occasion. He's after something, and thinks you have it. He somehow tracked me, of all people, and may have followed me here. But I dare say he's after you."

He checked his watch, scanned the street, then checked it again. Why that seemed sinister, I can't tell you. Maybe it was because I remember Simon Tingle doing the same thing before he was shot. I cast a quick look around for a car with no license plates. It wasn't there. Not yet.

179

Roald said, "This will sound odd, Sir Felix, but we have information that there will be an attempt on someone's life, possibly right here."

"Two attempts," Wade added. "Tonight."

Sir Felix blinked as if we were lunatics. Then he slid into gear. "I suggest some of you go inside and find whatever this man wants. Roald, Sara, you come with me and talk to my man in charge. Give him a description of your pursuers."

The church was open, dimly lit when we entered.

"Becca, are you sure about this?" asked Darrell as we crossed the nave.

I tried to reconnect the last few dots that had brought us there, but they wouldn't come together. "I don't know. I hope so, but I don't know." I shivered, my clothes still wet. My pulse pounded in my wrists, my neck, my temples. My forehead burned. I hoped something was down there we'd all missed the first time. If it wasn't, we had nothing.

We entered through the door at the base of the tower, picked through the rubble to the second door, and climbed the steps down into the crypt. Lily shed her tablet's full light ahead through the dust on Holbein's stone and the recently pried-out mortar around it.

"Lily, shine the light lower," I said, and read the writing on Joan Aleyn's partially pried-out stone.

JOAN ALEYN HOLBEIN
ORPHAN, FOUNDLING, WIFE
BORN 21 DECEMBER 1515

I felt myself sharpen, all my senses come into play. Maybe that's what saving a life does to you, puts you into focus. *If* I really did save Joan's life.

I reached out and placed my fingers on the stone. It was cold, damp. My fingertips searched for the words and numbers I had seen only an hour before.

DROWNED 6 JULY 1535

But they weren't there now, no matter what Markus Wolff and I had seen earlier. They weren't there. I stared at the stone. "She didn't . . . she didn't . . ."

"Becca?" Wade said. "What does it mean? No death date? But we saw it."

"It can't mean she's still . . ." Darrell didn't finish.

My heart shuddered inside my chest. All I could think was that I actually *had* tampered with history, that Joan Aleyn didn't die that day.

"She lives," I said. "Copernicus said, 'She lives.' He meant that Joan survived that night."

"It's not possible," Lily whispered. "It's not. But . . ."

I was already searching for another stone, the one I

181

now believed would be there. It was. Below Joan's vault was a third stone. It read:

REBECCA ALEYN HOLBEIN
DAUGHTER OF HANS AND JOAN HOLBEIN
BORN 7 SEPTEMBER 1535
DIED 19 MARCH 1604

"Rebecca Aleyn Holbein," Darrell whispered. "*R-A-H.* We didn't see that before."

"Because it wasn't there before," I said, shaking, terrified, and humbled that Joan had named her daughter after me. "The relic is behind Rebecca's stone. We have to open it. I don't want to, but we have to. Joan would want us to."

Together Wade and Darrell used the same tool Wolff had used earlier. They chipped away the mortar and carefully pried back the stone. A flat wooden box lay just inside, next to a tight wrapping of cloths and dust that might have been Rebecca's remains. My hands shook; my throat tightened. "Oh . . ."

Wade touched my arm. "Becca . . ."

I took control of myself and placed my hands on the box. It was made of wood and slate and clamped with brass corners. I brought it out into Lily's light. Lifting

182

the latch, we opened the box. Our faces were bathed in a fierce amber glow like Thomas More's had been five hundred years ago. I felt the same sort of quiet falling over us as in the cave on Guam when Wade and I found our first relic. The silence in the crypt just then was heavy, deep, almost holy.

And all too momentary.

The two equal arms of the cross begged to be attached.

"I think you should . . . ," said Wade, half reaching to pull wet hair from my cheeks, then letting his hand fall without doing it. It was such a different look from the one he gave me this morning. "You deserve to. You found it."

Lily and Darrell both nodded. I lifted out the two pieces. There was a notch in the center of each. I brought them together there. The arms sank into place with a click. The amber cross quivered in my hands for a moment, I let go, and rods suddenly jutted out of the arms, like multiple blades. Crux began to revolve in the air in front of us, like some kind of medieval helicopter. The two arms spun in opposite directions, making a strange, keening wail that grew louder and louder until Crux became its own winged machine. The cross of Copernicus, the prisoner's cross of Thomas More, the cross encrypted into the Holbein portrait, beamed out like a floodlight and lifted up to the ceiling of the chamber.

"Take it apart!" Lily said. "Take it apart! Guys—"

Both boys thrust their hands at the cross and carefully detached one wing from the other. The moment they set them back into the algorism box and closed it tight, the light vanished, and the muffled noise of life rushed back.

Wade's expression was of awe. We all must have looked the same.

"We have the relic," he said.

We did have the relic. Our second relic. We were in the lead once more.

Then we heard glass crashing on the floor above us.

CHAPTER TWENTY-TWO

I spun around toward the door at the top of the crypt stairs. "What was—"

Something shattered in the nave. Chairs, tables scraped across the floor. Then two pops of gunfire, and someone shouted, "Take him down! Everyone now!" A stampede of feet thundered across the church floor.

"Should we stay here?" Lily whispered. "I'm staying here. Sir Felix and his agents will protect us."

A flurry of more shots was followed by a pair of running feet toward the door from the nave into the tower. The door slammed aside while Darrell shut the door to the crypt and bolted it as Markus Wolff had done that afternoon.

We turned off our phone lights. Holbein's box was

already in my bag. We held our breath. Someone stepped through the debris outside our door. We leaned and ducked away from any line of fire. There was a knock instead.

"Hello, are you in there? This is Felix Ross. Your parents are safe, but Wolff is here, and that other man, Doyle. MI5 are cornering them, but you'd better slip out now, just in case."

We looked at one another in the dark. Wade whispered, "I guess it's all right."

Darrell climbed the stairs and unbolted the door; we opened it. Sir Felix was there, his friendly face half smiling. "Good show. Now, quietly. Very." He pressed a finger to his lips, turned, and started back. We followed him out one by one.

Only we didn't get far. Three steps outside of the crypt door, I felt cold metal pressing the back of my neck. "Don't move, you little thief!"

Everyone turned to see who was behind me. But I knew.

"Doyle!" I said.

"At your service. Your *funeral* service, that is. Now hand it over!" He kept the barrel pressed against my neck. I saw Sir Felix sizing up Doyle, as if he was thinking of a plan to help us, but without a gun, what could he do?

"I think we'd better do as he requests," he whispered. "Doyle, you *are* rather surrounded by British intelligence, poor chap. Nowhere to run, you see."

The killer snorted. "I *do* see. Once Wolff gets here, we'll *all* see. He picks off British intelligence for breakfast. Now give me the relic!"

Sir Felix urged the others away from Doyle and me, but as he did, someone pounded on the door to the nave—which Doyle must have locked—and the gunman turned his head. That's when Wade jumped forward and dragged the bag off my shoulder. He spun around, and instead of unlocking the door, he scrabbled across the rubble and hooked his arm around a broken beam slanting overhead. He pulled himself up to the third step of the tower and from there to the fourth.

"Why, I oughta—" Doyle shouted. He plowed through us, knocking Sir Felix to the stones, wriggling away from Darrell. He jumped up after Wade.

"It'll collapse!" I said. "Wade, stop!"

But he wouldn't. He was on what remained of the first landing and starting up on stairs even more rotten. Doyle was only a few steps behind him. I lost them both in the dark, then saw them in the lights from the upper windows. The wood must have sliced Wade's fingers. He slipped back. I screamed.

I couldn't watch and do nothing. I pushed away from

the others and hoisted myself up to the third step. My wounded arm burned, but I managed to clutch the next stair. I saw Wade kicking at Doyle, when Doyle's gun went off.

Plaster exploded off the ceiling, and white dust rained down on them. Doyle lowered his head. I slipped down, but caught myself. The whole staircase was sagging away from the wall now. I felt like throwing up, but I kept climbing.

Downstairs, the church was chaotic: people were pounding on the nave door but not getting it open. What had Doyle done to it?

Then, I don't know how, I was up there, too, battering Doyle's legs, then his back, then his head. He crumpled forward into Wade, pushing him against a window. I heard glass crack, then shatter in the street below. Wade's alarm, still on his belt loop, went off as he hit the window. Shouts came from the street.

I clasped both hands together and brought them down on Doyle's head. He fell forward. Wade threw his arms out, then twisted aside, his tinny alarm still beeping. Doyle went headfirst into the remaining glass, shrieked, and fell.

Out of the tower.

I screamed something I don't remember. Wade spun to the window. I climbed the last step and looked out next to him. Archie Doyle's body was twisted, facedown on the ground, surrounded by intelligence agents. I grabbed Wade to steady me.

"One dead," he said, his voice barely audible.

"No! What are you doing? No!" Lily yelled from below.

"I beg your pardon, I have to . . ." Strangely, Sir Felix was grappling for the stairs now. He was stronger than he looked and was already on the third step.

"We'll come down," I said, shaking, not knowing how I could make my feet move. But Sir Felix kept climbing up. The framework of the stairs shuddered. The weight was too much after all. The planks creaked beneath our feet.

"Yes, you'll come down," Sir Felix said. "Just like Archie did."

"Becca—" Wade said.

I watched the man's hand dip into his jacket. He withdrew something black.

"He's got a gun!" Darrell shouted, battering the locked door with a brick.

There was nothing to do, nowhere to go. Sir Felix was up there in no time.

"Archie Doyle was a bit of a fool, but a necessary one," he said, holding his gun on us, pushing us away from the window. We practically stepped on each other's toes. He peered out the window. "Simon Tingle, too. I naturally heard everything you asked him about. Both men, alas, won't see tomorrow."

"My dad says Simon will live," said Wade. "You won't get him."

"Won't I? A knight of the British Empire *and* of the Teutonic Order can do a great many things. The relic, please. Now there's a good fellow—"

Suddenly, the door broke open below us, and Roald and Terence, along with several agents, poured into the tower, shining powerful lights up at us.

"Sir Felix, you won't escape," one of the agents yelled. "Sir—"

The window behind Sir Felix exploded. Glass splashed inside the tower like water. Felix didn't have a chance to look around before a second blast blew him off the platform and out the window he'd just looked out of. Blew him out. As if he were a puppet.

I screamed and screamed.

"Omigod!" Lily cried out from below. "Who's shooting?"

Wade tried to hold me back, but I stepped to the edge of the sagging floor and looked out the glassless window frame. "Becca, get out of the way—"

On the scaffolding of the building across the street, I glimpsed a shape in a long leather coat. There was the brief glint of a gun barrel, a flash of white hair, then nothing. "It's over," I said. I knew the shooting was over. Two were dead. There wouldn't be any more tonight. Copernicus had told me what to expect.

"Wolff's appointment. He was after Sir Felix."

Leadenhall was a carnival of flashing lights and men with automatic weapons. Two crumpled bodies lay on the street not far from each other. Medical personnel crowded around them, but they were clearly dead.

Two dead in the shadow of the tower.

Even without seeing him, I knew that a man who didn't belong in that sudden crowd was down there. Someone from another time.

Nicolaus Copernicus.

Had he seen all this before, or was he seeing it now? If he *was* seeing it now, was he still on his unexplained third journey? Or was this his fourth, or eighth, or tenth? No answers came. Time was shot through with holes.

One thing I knew: history was already changing. Because I had saved Joan Aleyn? Or because I didn't break Markus Wolff's phone when I had the chance?

Holodomor. Yellow Turban.

The names of those tragedies swam in my head. How could one person do so much horror? What horrors were beginning right here and now?

Someone was pulling me. Wade. Wade was pulling me back down the stairs. "I was scared," he said. "That we'd lose you."

I gripped his hand as hard as I could. "Me, too."

My heart was stuffed in my throat. Barely able to breathe, I wanted to bury myself in him and the others and not let go and not have to say anything. I knew that eventually I would have to talk about it. But not right now. I didn't know the right words. Only the wrong ones.

Uskok . . . Smyrna . . .

So that's pretty much the unfunny story I promised you.

Ha. Ha. Ha.

Except it's not the *whole* story.

CHAPTER TWENTY-THREE

Friday, March 28
9:28 a.m.

Last night, after everything we had done, my sleep was black, deep, and dreamless.

Nearly dreamless.

Sometime during the long night, I caught a glimpse of Joan, stumbling away on the dark sand to find Hans Holbein, the father of her child. The weight of early death had been lifted from her. I also saw Helmut Bern sailing to a monastery, heading for Kronos. I prayed he'd find it before the microhole closed.

I had no idea what horrors would happen because of what I had done, but neither of those two things seemed bad. It was only later, at Heathrow this morning, that the final puzzle piece clicked into place.

At the Pret A Manger in Terminal 3.

***

My parents had texted last night to say that they'd found seats on an evening flight out from Austin. As we waited now for the plane that would bring Lily's father and my parents and Maggie to us, we quietly worked out yesterday's events. The passage of Crux from Nicolaus to Thomas and then on the day of Thomas's death to Meg and Joan, and later to Joan's daughter, Rebecca. How Sir Felix had appeared as Hatman at the embankment yesterday morning, how he had planted the bug on my bag in his office, how he had worked with Doyle, how Wolff had finally taken him out, and how the Teutonic Order was cruel to its own.

My nose hadn't bled for hours, but unprepared as I always am, when I talked about Joan at the river, I had to use a table napkin to dry what I hoped would be my last round of tears. Or I would have dried them, if I hadn't stopped dead.

When I brought the Pret A Manger napkin to my face, I finally noticed the funny little recycling comment printed on it.

If Pret staff . . . hand you huge bunches of napkins (which you don't need or want) please give them the evil eye. Waste not want not.

I grew cold all over and realized what had really happened.

. . . the evil . . .

Because of the strange coilings of time, I had left something behind at the river nearly five hundred years ago. Joan Aleyn had kept the napkin I'd used to stop her bleeding forehead and put it in the locket that contained her husband's portrait of her. I couldn't tell you why Markus Wolff had the locket, but secreted inside it was the napkin that had mingled Joan's and my blood together. The napkin that Nicolaus somehow must have known about. The napkin that memorialized why Joan had named her daughter after me.

Copernicus had said it was good that she lived.

Yes, it was.

But then, what did *the evil* mean? Had a horrible thing already happened sometime in the past? Was it evil that Helmut Bern found his way back to Kronos? Would it have been better if Joan had died that night?

I knew I wouldn't have done anything different.

And why was Galina so obsessed with this mute girl in the first place? So much so that she sent her best agent to find out about her? What did Joan Aleyn *really* mean to Galina Krause? Were she and Galina related, as Wolff had suggested? Was *that* what this was all about? Blood?

Or more accurately . . . *bloodline*?

Only then did I understand that we—all of us—are as deeply woven into the protection of the Legacy as Copernicus himself was. We are part of his Legacy, tangled up and bound to it like he himself was—and is.

We make the horror happen. We make the good.

Copernicus swore a deadly oath to protect the world from a horror without end, and we are bound to swear that oath, too. Have I caused tragedies? Maybe. But aren't we causing tragedies every moment of our lives? Aren't we all blind men, setting fire to everything we touch? Have I gone into the past? Or has the past come forward for me? Is there any difference between the past and the present? And what about the future? Where— and when—*is* the future, exactly?

I daubed my eyes, then crunched the napkin and threw it away.

As the plane from Austin landed and we crowded together to see my parents and Maggie, I knew one thing at least. In my bag, nestled close to Copernicus's diary, was Holbein's wooden box. And inside the box lay the prisoner's cross.

We had Crux.

We were winning.

Two to one.

ACKNOWLEDGMENTS

Gratitude goes to many people who helped in the writing of this book, from the technical to the inspirational. In the first category is the National Trust Photo Library in England, whose splendid staff I contacted regarding Rowland Lockey's 1592 portrait of Thomas More's family, an image after a lost Holbein original. Readers can study this image for the hidden cross referred to in the story.

A hearty thank-you goes to the staff at HarperCollins UK, with whom I enjoyed a fine lunch in Hammersmith by the ever-present Thames, and especially to Ruth Alltimes and Sarah Radford; also to Tania Fitzgerald at Historic Royal Palaces for even entertaining a request to visit the Bell Tower—on Good Friday, of all days. I promise proper notice next time.

To Tony, the real buildings manager at Saint Andrew Undershaft, and John Ewington, OBE, at Saint Katharine Cree, thank you both for letting me poke around your churches, though certainly not to the extent described in this book.

Visitors to Bletchley Park will already know the magic of the place. Since the beginning of this series I've wanted to set part of the Copernicus story there, and I'm happy to have had the opportunity. The men and women who worked there in the period between 1939 and 1945 are, as we now know, very real heroes. To say that I want to live and work at Bletchley during those years would remain no more than an idle dream—except for the possibilities suggested by this book. I'll keep hoping. During my visit, in addition to benefiting from the docent's fine description of the Enigma machine, I was honored to meet one of the original Wrens, the sparkly Joan Martin—"Lewis, when I was here." If I have given my Bletchley character the name Mavis, I have also given her Mrs. Martin's resonant words to me: "I worked on the Bombe, you know. The *Turing* Bombe."

Within the terms of this very short novel, I've tried to stick with as many facts as I could. Thomas More's life and death, his letters, his family, and his love for Meg are well known. Nicolaus Kratzer, Hans Holbein, and Joan Aleyn are real. Some facts—the shadiness of Kratzer, for example, or the dates of Holbein's actual residency in England—have been adjusted for this story. My playfulness with minor points of recorded history do not, of course, reflect on any of my outstanding sources. Of those many I want to single out *The Life of Thomas More* by Peter Ackroyd, *Wolf Hall*, the novel by Hilary Mantel, *The Secret Lives of Codebreakers* by Sinclair McKay, *Hans Holbein: Revised and Expanded Second Edition* by Oskar Bätschmann and Pascal Grenier, and *Saint Thomas More: Selected Writings* edited by John F. Thornton and Susan B. Varenne, with a preface by Joseph W. Koterski. The latter two volumes are quoted here, the first in reference to the likely location of Holbein's tomb, the second in the excerpts from More's last letter.

Gratitude, as always, to my wife, Dolores, for her close readings and suggestions; to my dear editor, Claudia Gabel; and to Katherine Tegen, Melissa, Alana, Ro, Lauren, my splendid copy editor Karen, and everyone else at KT Books and HarperCollins who make these stories live. Thank you, all.